Lilac Skully and the Haunted House

Book #1

In The Supernatural Adventures of Lilac Skully

Lilac Skully and the Haunted House

Amy Cesari

1.

A Terrible Night in Skully Manor

Lilac had been peering out of the curtains for half an hour. The rain was increasing in intensity. Flashes of lightning illuminated the dark woods behind Skully Manor. Something touched her hand, and she jolted backward, quickly realizing it was just her cat. Casper hopped up onto the window seat and nestled his head underneath her hand.

"It's been almost two weeks now," Lilac said to Casper matter-of-factly, breaking her own silence. She moved several books off of the blanket and pulled it over herself. She curled up on the small padded bench by the window. Casper sat on top of her lap, and Lilac stroked his head.

"Father's note said it might be *a while...*" she emphasized those two words slowly and carefully, thinking to herself of all the different things that "*a while*" could mean if she thought about it.

But two weeks was longer than she had expected. Much longer.

She'd thought her father meant "*a while*" as in just a

few hours. Maybe leaving her alone from early morning till night on the same day, as he had done a few times before.

Yet the hours of his first day gone turned into overnight. Lilac awoke the next morning, startled to see that her father was not there. Two days turned into three. Then, a week. And now, if she counted correctly, thirteen days had passed since her father had left.

She took out the note from under the cushion and clicked on the flashlight. The dim, yellowing bulb illuminated Lilac from below, making her look even stranger than normal.

Her hair was striking white-blonde, stick straight and thin. Her large, deep-set grey eyes were round and kind of a funny shape on the outer sides. And with the shadows from the flashlight, her eyes looked even bigger and weirder. Not quite ten years old, she was odd, yet strangely pretty. Her looks had always drawn heaps of unwanted attention. Stares, questions, and comments like, "Oh my gosh, look at that strange little girl," all of which made Lilac terribly uncomfortable. Apparently, she looked just like her mother. But Lilac didn't remember her mother. She had only seen a couple of photographs, and although Lilac saw the resemblance, she still felt like there wasn't anyone else that looked as weird as her.

She read her father's letter again, but she'd read it so many times before. She knew it word by word.

Lilac,

Excuse me for leaving so suddenly. There is urgent business to which I must attend, and I may be gone a while. Do not leave the house, and do not answer the door for anyone.

-Father

She sighed and folded up the note, stuffing it back under the cushion and clicking off the flashlight.

"I *never* leave, and I *never* answer the door, anyway," she said to herself, dismissing what her father had instructed. It was true, and Lilac preferred it that way for the most part. Her experiences of trying to settle in at different schools had all been awful. Several years ago, her father gave up and put her into home correspondence courses.

And no, she hadn't missed anything in his letter, she reassured herself. It offered no more clues about when he was returning than it did the first time she read it. She lay in the darkness and stared up at the ceiling, listening to the rain. Nope, not the slightest tone of affection anywhere in this hastily scribbled letter. Just like always. Short, curt, borderline flustered—and emotionless towards her.

She tried to tell herself that he was "just that way." Maybe she was silly that she thought he should write, "Dear Lilac," at the beginning, and, "Love, Father" at the end.

"I guess it really makes no difference that he's gone," she said out loud. She put her hand out and felt for Casper, who was curled up next to her. "I never see him much, anyway."

The wind howled. Lilac sat up and looked outside again. The trees were bending and swaying, their branches like arms waving desperately for help. She closed the curtains.

"The storm is really starting to come up," Lilac whispered. Casper sat, silent and unbothered, his eyes half closed.

Lilac was trying to pretend she didn't hear the house creaking in the wind. But she did. Lilac wanted to ignore all of the incredibly creepy things about living at Skully Manor—which was impossible—because Skully Manor was a haunted house.

Only a few years after the towering manor was built in 1867, there were a series of gruesome murders inside. Several families moved in and out quickly over the next decade, none of them able to withstand the hauntings and tragic energy that still lingered in the home. It then sat empty and unused for nearly twenty years, with absolutely no one interested in living there.

That was, until it was purchased by Lilac's great-grandfather, Mortimer Skully, a renowned paranormal investigator, who was thrilled at the prospect of moving into a haunted house. Lilac's family had now lived in the house for four generations. It had become known as Skully Manor, the most haunted house in town.

When Lilac thought about it, which was often, there were a lot of things she didn't like about living there. And it wasn't just the ghosts that tormented her mercilessly if she stepped foot into the main house.

She detested the cold chills that blew through the walls. Not just when the wind howled, but anytime the spirits came out to haunt. She disliked that the house was so large and ancient, and that all of the furniture and things inside it were at least a hundred years old. She abhorred the poltergeist in the cellar. She couldn't stand the moldy, musty smells that made her sneeze. She didn't like the thistles in the garden, or the fact that the house overlooked a large, overgrown cemetery on the edge of town. She was creeped out by the spiders, both living and dead, and the decades worth of cobwebs and creepy little nests that filled every nook and cranny. Sometimes she felt like there might be thousands of tiny spider eyes watching her.

Yet she still felt alone, which was perfectly fine with her, she reasoned. She preferred to be alone. Alone except for her cat and a handful of ghosts that she tried her best to avoid. And her father, of course, until he left suddenly thirteen days ago, and still hadn't returned.

The wind came up again, and the manor house wailed, creaked, cracked, and moaned.

Bang.

Her whole body jumped, and she froze. That was not one of the "ordinary" sounds that haunted Skully Manor. Lilac Skully knew the sounds of the ghosts well. She heard another great bang and clatter out in the main hall.

Bang! Clatter!

Lilac nearly jumped out of her skin, every cell of her body freezing into a panic midair. Casper was jolted awake and flung upwards. His claws caught on the blanket clumsily, legs stiff and outstretched. He quickly sensed danger and scurried into his usual nook under the china cabinet.

Lilac wondered if it was better to stay perfectly still or to move and hide under the blanket. Should she blink? Close her eyes? Leave them open?

Thunder roared, and then again, *Bang!*

This time the noise jolted her up enough that she could also throw the blankets over herself in the confusion of the moment. She clenched the blanket down over her, hoping to disappear, hoping that whatever it was, it would just stop.

Bang! Bang! She heard the sounds again and flattened herself down more into the crack between the cushions and the window seat, as if to become a part of the furniture.

Bang! Bang! Bang! It was her heart. It was more like a thump, but she could hear it quite loudly.

Bang!

It was almost as if someone was banging at the door, but Lilac knew it wasn't that. The sound of someone rapping at the knocker on the front door was a sound Lilac knew all too well.

Bang! Bang! It continued. It was definitely not the front door.

Bang! Bang! Bang! It did not stop.

She lay motionless for a moment and all sorts of terrible scenarios ran through her mind.

The sound was coming from upstairs. But this wasn't the same kind of deathly, wailing sound that usually haunted the halls up there. This banging noise was getting louder as the wind blew, and it reverberated throughout the walls of the entire manor. If it wasn't the door, and it wasn't a typical haunting, then what could it be?

"The shutters!" Lilac suddenly realized, whispering aloud to herself, deep in her cocoon of blankets. "It's just the shutters!"

Relieved that the sound probably wasn't paranormal, she came out from under the blankets. Her body warmed, and she felt the tension subside.

The old wooden shutters on the front of the house were notorious for banging about if you didn't latch them. It was something her father took care of, or more likely, would forget, and then have to deal with in the middle of the night during the first storm of the year.

And that's what was happening right now, Lilac reasoned. Except her father wasn't there to take care of it. She was on her own.

It was one of the rare moments where Lilac wished she had someone to call for help. But she didn't. As scared as Lilac was living inside Skully Manor, she was even more scared to go out. The world had been cruel to Lilac Skully in the nine-and-three-quarter years of her life so far, and even though her house was horrifying, it felt safer to her than anywhere else.

Bang. Bang. Bang. She wished she could ignore it. But she knew she wasn't going to be able to sleep with the shutters banging, or worse, if the shutters slammed so hard that the windows broke, she'd be in big trouble. She'd have to call someone. A repair man. A stranger. She shuddered. The storm and wind were just going to get worse through the next day. They had said so on the local news. She knew she had to go up there and deal with it.

"It's just as well," she sighed and folded her arms, gathering up her gumption and logical reasoning.

"While I'm up there, I can get some warmer things from my room."

Lilac could feel the seasons shifting quickly. It was getting cold, and there were some sweaters, coats, hats, blankets, socks, and woolen tights from upstairs that she wished she had.

"I'll just go up there as fast as I can and latch the shutters," she said out loud, knowing she had to start talking herself into it sooner or later.

But there was no "just" going upstairs for Lilac Skully. She was terribly afraid of ghosts. And walking the halls of the haunted manor in the middle of a stormy night—or even in the day—was something that Lilac avoided at all costs.

She had spent the majority of her childhood refusing to sleep in her own bedroom or use the rooms in the main part of the house unless absolutely necessary. Instead, Lilac lived in the old maid's quarters off the back of the kitchen. This section of the house had been added on after the hauntings began, and Lilac had never seen a ghost there. It was cozy, about the size of a closet with a small washroom, but Lilac had decorated it with paper chains, dolls, drawings, and of course, her books in the nearby pantry. She had everything she needed, and hadn't left the kitchen and maid's quarters at all in several months.

It drove her father crazy. He'd been raised at Skully Manor too, he'd tell Lilac, exasperated, as if living with documented poltergeists was perfectly normal. He was a third-generation paranormal investigator, he'd tell her, as if Lilac was ridiculous for feeling how she felt, just because he was nuts. But Lilac was still afraid and stayed tucked away despite her father's objections. The maid's quarters and kitchen felt like home. She was safe. As long as she didn't venture into the main part of the house. Or worse, go down into the cellar.

She gulped. Just the thought of going down to the cellar made Lilac queasy. But it had just crossed her mind. Lilac knew that sooner or later—if her father did not return—she would have to go down there. She was running out of supplies in the pantry—including the food she had for herself and the canned fish that she fed to Casper. She had been putting it off for a while now, even though she knew that, in the cellar, there was more sugar for her tea, as well as a case of orange soda, and even peanut butter and jam to go with her dwindling supply of crackers.

But the basement of Skully Manor was haunted by a terrible poltergeist, Mr. Fright. His name in life had been Fredrick Wright, yet like all of the ghosts in the manor, he'd become so famous in his death that he'd earned himself a nickname. Fright.

She folded over herself at the edge of the bed and rested her head in her hands. She wondered if she'd rather go without food than go down into the cellar and deal with Mr. Fright. Probably. She sighed. Just the thought of him made a cold chill rush through her. She tried to shake it off. She didn't have to worry about Mr. Fright right now. Maybe not even tomorrow. She had enough cans of fish and food to make it through a day or two. Didn't she?

"At the most." she said to herself under her breath.

Bang. Bang. Bang. Her thoughts of impending woe were interrupted by the shutters, still banging in the wind. She stood up, fists clenched to her sides, and nodded her head a bit, with as much confidence as she could muster.

"I have to do this!" Lilac said. "I'll just run upstairs to latch the shutters. And if I can, I'll grab the warmer clothes and blanket of out my room." She nodded again and thought reassuring things.

"If I see a ghost or anything weird happens," she reasoned, "I'll forget the clothes and just run back down after I latch the shutters."

Bang. Bang. Bang. The wind blew, and the shutters clanged and shook the old bones of Skully Manor harder with each bluster.

Lilac went to the pantry shelf and waved her fingers in the air as she looked for a particular book. She had amassed a wide selection of books in there. It was a large walk-in pantry that had been suitable for manor life with a big family. But since just Lilac, her father, and her cat lived at Skully Manor—and the ghosts—there wasn't a need for a large stock of food. Most of the shelves were empty all of the time. So Lilac had filled several of them with books, any books she could get her hands on, from famous and not-so-famous literary works to an old encyclopedia set, antique comic books, and various works of nonfiction that she'd been able to collect over the years.

She pulled out a small purple book with gold-leaf lettering, *How to Work With Ghosts* by Mathias Thimbleweed. She sat on a stool at the kitchen counter and flipped straight to the back of the book. On the last page, it read in Lilac's own handwriting:

How to AVOID Ghosts.
By Lilac Skully.

If you see a ghost, run.
If a ghost sees you, run.
If you feel a ghost, run.
If you sense a ghost, run.
If you hear a ghost, run.

If you HAVE TO go into the Manor:
- Wear sneakers with rubber soles.
- Double knot laces.
- Cover your skin! You'll be less likely to feel the creepy crawlies if you have layers on.
- Pants under a skirt is a good option.
- Always wear a hat or a hood.
- Bring the crystal medallion for protection.
- Put a clove of garlic, some lilacs, or frankincense in your pocket.

"Lilacs," she laughed and sighed a little, shaking her head. She'd always thought that was ironic. Her name was Lilac. But Lilacs were supposed to protect you from spirits. Yet there she was, surrounded by ghosts who scared her.

She went through the checklist items, one by

one, putting on her sneakers with double knots and a thin rain jacket with the hood tied tight. She tucked her pajama pants into her socks. She took the crystal medallion and lilac sachet out of her wooden treasure box and put them both in her jacket pocket.

Bang. Bang. Bang. The shutters banged again and reverberated through the walls and Lilac's bones with each clash.

She closed her eyes and visualized her plan. She was going to run. As fast as she could. Straight out of the kitchen and through the house. Then up the stairs. Once upstairs, she would waste no time. She would find the clanging shutters and fix them, she reckoned. She gulped and shook off the goose bumps.

The Hall of the Little Girl Ghost was on the second floor. It was one of the most famous haunted locations in town. It was also the hall that led to Lilac Skully's bedroom—the one she didn't use anymore. As you can imagine, the ghost in the hall was a big reason why Lilac preferred to live downstairs.

"The windows get stuck," she remembered, continuing through her mental list, "especially when it rains." This was true. "Good point," she praised herself.

"Use all your strength," she instructed, confidently, nodding her own head in agreement.

She remembered that some of the large double-hung windows had broken sash cords, which meant they wouldn't stay open. She might have to prop them open with a piece of wood as she did downstairs. She grabbed the large wooden stick that she used as a window prop. Although she knew it couldn't protect her from ghosts, carrying a big stick gave her some confidence anyway.

"You never know," she told herself, brandishing her stick.

"I'll be right back," she knelt down and reached under the old china cabinet to pet her sandy white cat.

Before she ran out of courage, she unlatched the locks and latches on the kitchen doors. She cleared her throat. She took a deep breath. She stepped back a few paces, got a running start, and pushed through the double doors.

Straight into the main house of notoriously haunted Skully Manor.

2.

The Hall of the Little Girl Ghost

Lilac burst through with a clatter, both doors swung wide and hit back against the wall as she sprinted across the dining room. A massive thunderbolt struck nearby. The sudden roar caused Lilac to gasp, trip, and fall. The flashing lightning made her think aliens might be attacking, at least for a split second. Her wooden stick dropped from her hands onto the cold marble floor with another loud clatter. She got up without hesitation and kept running, out of the dining hall and through the foyer of the old manor.

Lightning and thunder struck again as she ran up the stairs at full speed, with a sudden burst of fearlessness.

Bang, Bang. Bang. The shutters banged as she got closer to the hallway. She had been correct. It was just the shutters. Now, she only had to latch them, grab some warm clothes, and get back to the kitchen.

Bang. Bang. Flash. Another thunderbolt and flash of lightning shook the roof and illuminated the long hallway in front of Lilac. Lilac tried not to look directly down the hall. If the Little Girl Ghost was there, she didn't want to see her, or worse, lock eyes.

The wind blew again. *Bang.* She saw that only one of the shutters was loose. Lilac tried to open the window's latch, but it was rusted shut. Her small fingers couldn't turn it. As hard as she tried, it wouldn't budge.

She tried the next window, hoping she could climb out and crawl over. The latch on the second window opened easily enough, but the wooden frame had swollen tight in the rain. Lilac pushed with all her might, bending her knees and using her whole body to try and open it.

Bang. Bang. Bang. The shutters were loud from downstairs, but from up here, they were deafening. *Bang.*

She felt the old wood of the window begin to give and move just a bit. She pushed again till her arms and hands felt like they might break, and the stuck window pane finally jolted open. She propped it up with the stick and climbed out onto the overhang.

The rain was coming down in sheets, and the mossy, moldy, fanciful shingled roof was more slippery and sloped than it had looked from inside. Lilac got a terrible feeling about what she was going to do, but she did it anyway. She climbed out over the windowsill and onto the sloped roof of the second floor.

She instantly wished she hadn't. Her feet slid out

from under her. Her knees scraped hard against the shingles. Pieces of the cracked slate started to break off underneath her. She gasped and grabbed for the windowsill. Her hands slipped and began to lose their grip.

If she couldn't hold on, she would fall from the second story of Skully Manor. It was a harrowingly far distance, as Skully Manor loomed tall and ominous over the rest of the neighborhood.

Lilac tried to cry out, but no sound would come. Her legs dangled over the edge. She was unable to do anything else other than what her instincts told her to do. She hung on for dear life. She reminded herself that she'd made a terrible mistake and that she was about to meet a painful, tragic end to her young life. Or best, be gravely injured.

Her hands became increasingly slippery and sore. She wasn't sure if she could hold on much longer. She looked down and instantly regretted it.

This was it. She felt dizzy. Her hands were slipping. Maybe it would just be broken legs, she hoped, and someone would find her early enough in the morning.

"It's 3:00 a.m.," she said to herself and then counted forward the probable hours she'd have to lie there dying and in pain and agony before someone walked by and found her.

"Four, five, six, seven, eight, nine..." She didn't think anyone would be coming by until the mailman showed up. "ten..." she counted. This was it. She was going to die.

Her hand slipped. But then her left foot caught something. Or did something catch her? She hesitated for a split second as an eerie chill crept over her. She reasoned she must've stepped on an ornate piece of trim or perhaps a cornice or a loose gutter that just happened to be under her foot.

Whatever it was, she was able to grab the windowsill with a better grip, and pull her feet back up onto the roof. Her sneakers then slipped again on the wet mossy shingles, mercilessly and almost comically, one after another, as she tried to regain her footing. She threw her elbows up and over the windowsill, banging her arms painfully in the process, but getting a solid grip. She pulled herself up to her armpits, and then enough to get all the way over. She fell to the floor of the hall with a wet, gasping flop.

Bang. Bang. Bang. She still had not latched the shutters. She wanted to cry. But she could not spend all night or even one minute lying here in the Hall of the Little Girl Ghost.

She got up and took the wooden stick out of the open window and shut it.

She quickly thought up another plan. She would use the end of the stick as a hammer to try and open the latch of the first window.

Bang, bang, bang. She hammered the small, rusted thumb latch of the window with the big wooden stick. She thought she felt it budge. It did. She hit it again, and the latch opened.

"Yes!" she told herself, her confidence growing again. "Almost there," she whispered, shaking and soaking wet.

She propped the window up with the stick and then leaned over the windowsill as carefully as she could.

Bang. The wooden shutters on the front of the house were massive and likely more than half her weight. It was a big stretch for her arms to try and reach the hook while hanging on and not falling out of the window again.

She tried not to look down but accidentally got a glimpse out of the corner of her eye. If she fell, she'd likely be impaled, by the rusty and horrifically pointy wrought-iron fencing down below.

Bang. The shutter swung back against the house with such force that it pushed Lilac back in. She sprung back up, using one arm and leg to hold on for dear life, the other to get her out of the window far enough to latch the shutter. She could barely reach the eye-hook latch with the tips of her fingers, and by a stroke of luck, she flicked it, and the eye-hook fell right in.

"Yes!" she yelled out to herself. She tipped her head back into the sheets of cold rain and savored her victory for a moment. Lightning flashed nearby, illuminating her striking white hair and pale complexion, giving Lilac an unearthly glow in the night.

She began to wriggle herself back inside, her adrenaline running low as fatigue set in quickly. As she twisted herself back in, her foot kicked the stick propping up the window. The stick fell into the hall with a clatter, and the huge pane of the double hung window slammed down on top of Lilac.

Thwunk.

"Aaagh!" Lilac cried as the force of the wood-framed window pane fell onto her, hitting her shoulder and crushing her under its weight.

As the window compressed her chest, she found it harder and harder to draw a breath. She gasped and struggled. She was helplessly stuck, half in and half out of the window. Her head, left leg, left shoulder, and arm were outside. The window was pinning the rest of her down inside, and she could not seem to move any of her limbs in a way that would open the window back up. She tried to use her outside arm to lift up the window, but her position was too awkward, and she didn't have the leverage to free herself.

Worse, Lilac began to grow cold in a terribly familiar way. The hairs on her arms and legs stood on end, despite her carefully planned layers of clothing.

"Oh, no," she whispered to herself as her limbs started to shake and tremble uncontrollably. She tried again to free herself from the window, but she could not move. And by now, gravity had sunk the window down further and gotten her even more stuck.

"Liiiilac!"

She heard a faint voice call from inside.

"Liiiiiiiiii-laaaaaaaac..." the voice wailed.

Lilac's face twisted as she struggled with wide-eyed panic. For a moment, she wondered if she stayed still, maybe she wouldn't be seen. She quickly realized how ridiculous that was. She'd already been seen. The ghost was calling her name. She was trapped, stuck in an awkward and downright dangerous situation. Halfway out a second-story window of the notoriously haunted Skully Manor.

She looked through the window, into the house. She tried to breathe and felt herself go dizzy. Just on the other side of the glass, she saw the apparition of the Little Girl Ghost, coming straight towards her.

She flailed breathlessly and found the last bit of adrenaline she had left. She wriggled and pushed the window up with all her might. The window nudged up ever so slightly. She pushed again, and it gave her enough room to get better leverage and a little bit of momentum.

With her last burst of energy, she flung herself back into the hall and the window crashed down with a thunk, nearly crushing her foot.

Lilac fell to the floor of the hallway in a gasping wet heap.

"Liiii-laac!" She heard again.

Lilac looked up. There in front of her, stood the pale blue patent leather party shoes of the Little Girl Ghost.

"Liiiiiii-lac!" the Little Girl Ghost wailed, and the eerie little shoes and frilly socks took another ghostly step closer.

Time stood still. Lilac didn't think she could get any colder, but she did. And she didn't think she'd be able to move. She felt frozen. Her muscles had all seized up for good, she was certain.

"If you see a ghost, run! If a ghost sees you, run!" she recited from her book under panicked breath. "Three. Two. One." she counted down.

With every ounce of energy she could muster, somehow, she found herself moving. She ran. She ran back downstairs at the greatest speed she could through the foyer and across the dining hall. She slammed through the double doors of the kitchen with a clatter and horrible guttural scream, frightening Casper and sending him back under the china cabinet in a flurry. Her fingers shook violently as she tried to work the latches on the kitchen door. She wrestled and missed and struggled with the rusty old locks, finally getting them locked. She sprinted through the kitchen, flicked off the lights midair, and flung herself into the pile of books and blankets on her window seat.

Gasping for breath, Lilac threw the blankets over herself and crammed her body down in between the cushions and the side of the window.

Her heart thumped. The rain was still coming down in sheets. Thunder and lightning flashed and boomed in the distance.

Lilac lay perfectly still until her panic gave way to exhaustion, and she fell fast asleep.

3.

Fish and Crackers

When Lilac woke up, it was daylight. She looked outside and could see earthworms squiggling on the crooked cement path out back. It was still raining, but it had subsided from the peak of last night's storm.

She got up and made herself some hot tea. Although the maid's quarters she slept in were tiny, the large Victorian-era kitchen of the manor was spacious. It had towering high ceilings, like all of the rooms in the manor, and an enormous stone hearth fireplace against one wall. No one had used the fireplace in decades, and it was so big that the cooking stove had been installed inside of it. The hanging copper pots and pans had become so tarnished that they were a bright shade of sea green. A large wooden counter block occupied the center of the room, with two mismatched stools pulled up to it. All of the walls and built-in cabinets of the kitchen had been painted the dullest pea green. The paint was made even duller by the years of dust that covered everything in the house, so the kitchen always had a dim, eerie light to it, like it would glow in the dark when the lights went out. But it didn't.

She opened up the last can of fish for Casper.

"You'll use the good china today," she told him. She set out a quarter of the can on a very fancy bone china plate, hoping it would distract him from the much smaller portion of food.

She got out her breakfast, a dwindling box of dry crackers, and sighed.

The good thing about having a father like hers, she reckoned, was that he barely paid her any mind. She could be having orange soda, peanut butter, and jam with her crackers for breakfast, and her father wouldn't notice or care at all. He would have even gone down into the cellar to get the soda for her if she asked him enough times.

Lilac crunched her crackers and washed them down with water from the sink. She would have liked an orange soda right about now. She tried not to think about the peanut butter and jam in the basement.

She heard a tinkling noise and saw that it was Casper licking his plate. He'd licked it so clean, that he'd pushed it against his water dish.

Clink, clink, clink, the very fancy empty plate went as he licked it.

"Oh, Casper!" she sighed. She jumped off of her stool

and sat down on the creaky wooden floorboards.

"Meow?" His sandy, striped head perked up and tilted to the side a bit. He walked over and rubbed up against Lilac's leg.

"What am I doing?" She picked him up by his middle and hoisted him onto her lap. "You poor kitty," she said as she held his head, a bit to his dismay, and looked deep into his blue eyes.

"All you've got is your fish! And I'm holding it back from you and... and starving you because I'm just a big chicken that's afraid of the cellar!" She felt tears come to her eyes and let them fall for the first time since the harrowing experiences of the previous night.

Her shoulders shook as she sobbed. She held her cat on her lap and stroked his fur, wiping the tears away on her sleeve.

She *was* afraid of the cellar. And for good reason. When Mr. Fright haunted, it was often in the basement. And Mr. Fright was the kind of ghost that made even the most experienced paranormal investigators, mediums, and professional spirit workers run away in horror and sweaty panic.

He was thought to have been a man named Frederick Wright in life. Yet there were still many unsolved mysteries and conflicting legends about who Mr. Fright truly was while he was living—and why he haunted

Skully Manor so mercilessly for over a hundred years. But there was one thing that almost everyone knew about him while he was dead, and that was that he absolutely, positively, hated little girls.

And so, for Lilac Skully, who was a little girl growing up in the same house as Mr. Fright, going into the basement was even more terrifying, creepy, and unsettling than usual. And going into the cellar is always a little bit creepy it seems, no matter what.

Through tears, Lilac spoke to her cat and herself.

"I won't wait anymore. I've got to do something, for your sake at least," Lilac said. She hugged her cat tightly. He let her, although it was a bit tight for his liking.

"I'll get these ghosts to leave," she continued, "and if they don't leave, I'll just go into the basement anyway. I'll deal with Mr. Fright. And I'll get your fish, and I'll get stuff for myself, the orange soda and whatever else I want."

She got up and sat back at the counter, and took another sip of tea. She picked up the small purple book with faded gold leaf lettering, *How To Work With Ghosts*. The book was a reject from her father's paranormal research library. Her father said it was "hogwash" and was going to toss it out, but she took it for her book collection.

Instead of turning to the section she had written

herself in the back of *How to Work with Ghosts,* she read through the Table of Contents.

"Hmmm..." she muttered, stroking her finger over the page.

"How to Get Ghosts to Leave." She flipped to the proper chapter.

"The Basics... Séance... Exorcism... When to involve professional Clergy..."

She thumbed through the chapter and read aloud again, "The first thing you should try is simply asking the ghost to leave in a firm, strong voice." She looked up and rolled her eyes. "Well, I've tried that a million times," she said, shaking her head.

She had. To her father's annoyance and only when he was around for protection, she would stand in the hall and yell for the ghosts to leave. Hoping and believing that if she told them enough times, they would go away. But they didn't.

"Sometimes," she read on, "they can't hear you because the lines of communication between the living world and the spirit world are closed." She stopped and looked up, her lower lip jutting out as she nodded her head.

"Often, a séance is performed first to open the lines of communication with the spirit world," she read. Interesting. She flipped through another couple of pages.

"How to have a séance," she continued. "First, create an environment that's comfortable and inviting for the spirits." She stopped reading.

"Inviting?" she said to Casper, "I want them to leave!" She shook her head but read on.

"In a room where the ghosts haunt, set up a table with some candles and sage or other incense to burn." She paused and glanced toward the pantry. "I think I've got all that."

She continued to read again. "Begin your séance at midnight," She stopped. "Midnight?! Ugh." She closed the book and set her chin in her hands, elbows propped on the counter. She had imagined doing this in broad daylight. That would be scary enough in Skully Manor.

She sat quietly for a few moments and had some tea. She wondered if she could find some money somewhere in the house, and then buy more food instead of having to go down to the cellar. Casper came up and rubbed against her leg, then jumped onto the counter.

"Maybe this is a bad idea. Contacting the spirits?" She sipped her tea. "I mean, I guess what could go wrong?" Lilac sighed. Casper looked back up at her, blankly and hungrily.

The wind began to pick up again and there was a faint tremor of creaks through the walls of Skully

Manor. Lilac heard leaves blowing by outside, unable to hold on to the trees any longer.

She opened the book again and flipped back to where she'd left off.

"Begin your séance at midnight." she repeated and gulped. "Light your candles and incense," she read carefully.

"Circle your table three times, clockwise, imagining a circle of white light forming and protecting you from harm." She ran and grabbed a pencil and drew a star next to that part. It sounded especially important.

"Summon the spirits to join you in a clear, loud voice. There are no set words you need to say, but make sure your intentions are clear and simple. Something like, 'I call upon the spirits that reside here to join me. Can you hear me? Make yourself known!'"

She read through the instructions several times and then set the book down.

"Well, if I'm going to do this, I'm going to do this." She looked Casper in the eyes again and added, "Tonight."

Lilac spent the rest of the morning preparing for her séance, collecting some candles and matches, some sage from the pantry and a couple of old and yellowed tablecloths that no one had used in at least forty years. The instructions in the book clearly said it needed to look and feel inviting. She picked a few daisies and put them in a small vase. She dusted off some brass candleholders and anything else she could find that might look nice.

She put all of these items in a basket and set them by the large double doors of the kitchen. She felt determined in her decision, especially when lunch came around, and she remembered how sick she was of dry crackers.

Lilac spent her afternoon as she normally did, reading a bit, and eventually falling asleep for a nap around three o'clock. She slept longer than normal and awoke as the light of the day was fading fast. The woods behind her house had already darkened considerably. She started to feel a little queasy.

"Maybe it's not a good night for a séance," she said to Casper as the evening wore on. "What do you think?" she asked him. He didn't answer.

She double checked the pantry for cans of food that she might have missed. Maybe an extra box of crackers, mini sausages, or something else that she and Casper could eat for another day.

It had been two weeks since her father left. Maybe he'd come home tonight. He could walk in the door any moment and have takeout food to make up for his long, unexplained absence. Chinese, she thought. The thought of hot, spicy, delicious, flavorful food made her feel hungry.

She looked at Casper, who was licking the plate that he'd already licked clean hours ago at breakfast.

"Is it time for dinner?" she asked him. It was, he responded. She gave him a tiny portion of food and set out a few crackers for herself.

She reread the séance instructions one more time and managed to get herself fired up for an hour or so. But as the night wore on, so did her enthusiasm.

Restless and antsy, she tried to sleep. She set the alarm for 11:45 p.m., enough time to wake up, have some tea, and to bring her basket full of candles and supplies out into the main hall at midnight. But she couldn't sleep. She lay awake, unable to quiet her mind or squelch the uneasy feeling brewing in her stomach.

The alarm bell blared at 11:45 p.m., just as she had set it, and just as she had finally fallen asleep. It jolted her awake, and made her feel as if her heart would explode in her chest. She flew across the room, breathless, as her brain tried to catch up and figure out what had just happened. She realized it was the alarm. She turned off the blaring bell and tried to stay calm.

She shivered as she put on her nicest and warmest clothes. The book hadn't mentioned it, but since the séance was supposed to have an "inviting" atmosphere, she figured she'd dress for the occasion. She put on a long-sleeved velvet dress, cardigan, tights, and her rubber-soled sneakers—both laces tied in tight, double knots. The shoes would have to stay to code. She put on a fancy black Victorian hat that smelled like mold and the last whiff of an ancient perfume. She jumped up and down a few times and ran in place to try to get her blood pumping and warmed up. She put the crystal medallion around her neck and the sachet in her cardigan pocket.

"Just like the plan." she told herself out loud. "No time to worry. No turning back now." She put on the tea kettle. By the time she poured the boiling water over a bag of lemon tea, she was shaking so much that she spilled boiling water everywhere.

"Aaaah," she cried out as the hot water splashed onto her hand. She set down the kettle and picked up her cup and saucer. It was also shaking so hard that she had to set it back down. She sat on the stool and took some deep breaths. She looked at the clock.

11:53.

She took some more deep breaths. She opened up the purple book again and read through the séance instructions one more time, but her eyes just scanned over the page.

11:55.

She tried to think about something else. She closed

her eyes. She was in a light, bright cottage by the sea. She tried to imagine the salt air and a sunny day. She peered at the clock. 11:56. Her confidence was fading fast. She figured the time was close enough and she was ready to get it over with.

"Okay, Lilac." she said to herself in a tone much more enthusiastic than you usually hear out of Lilac Skully. "You're calm. You're cool. You're not afraid."

"This is your house," she continued, "you're in charge." She made a fist with one hand and slammed it into her other palm. "Sorry, ghosts, no, wait, not sorry..." She took a deep breath.

"Ghosts," she practiced calmly, "It's time for you to leave."

She unlocked the several locks and latches on the old double doors.

She picked up her basket with one hand, and with the other, pushed open the door. She stopped. A chilly and unsettling breeze blew in from the manor. Lilac got a whiff of a pale, sweet scent. It was the breeze that young Lilac knew all too well. It was a sign that the ghosts were out.

Lilac inhaled, and stepped through the door.

4.
The Sèance

Once Lilac had taken those first few steps into the dining hall, all of the nervousness vanished, and she felt a sudden sense of calm. It was like the time she was in public school for a few weeks and sang in the chorus recital. She was nervous all morning to the point of almost throwing up and going home sick, but once she stepped out onto the stage, she was surprisingly okay.

She walked through the dining hall and into the large foyer of Skully Manor. Since almost all of Skully Manor was haunted, she figured she'd do the séance in a central location. There was also a small round table that she thought she could push into the center of the room.

A bluish gray light from the stormy moon illuminated everything with a pale, eerie glow. Lilac flicked a switch to turn on the chandelier.

She set down her basket and tried to move the table. It was much heavier than she thought it would be. It had wrought-iron legs and a thick, marble top. It made loud, scraping, thunking noises as she dragged it across the room.

Screech. Screech. Screech, the metal feet scraped as Lilac scooted the table into the center of the foyer.

When she got it close enough, she set up the items she'd collected to make an inviting atmosphere. First, she laid out the yellowed tablecloths, one overlapping the other, just like the picture in the book.

She took out the tall, tarnished candlesticks and beeswax candles and arranged them as appealingly as possible. She put out the little vase of flowers which were already wilted. She set the purple book out on the table and opened it to the page about séances. Then she pulled over a tasseled stool so she'd have a place to sit.

Lilac struck a match and carefully lit one of the candles. She strode confidently back to the light switch and turned off the chandelier. A chill rushed through Skully Manor. The candle's eerie flicker cast strange shadows against the bluish gray glow of the moon. Her hand lingered on the switch, and she did not move. It suddenly felt like every inch of her body had seized up. She got the urge to abandon the séance and go back to the kitchen. To run and hide. She was only a few steps away from safety. She took a deep breath and pulled one foot off the floor. Her heartbeat was shaking her body with every pulse, which she tried to ignore, but she could not.

“There’s no such thing as ghosts,” she tried to tell herself. But she knew this wasn’t true at all. Her father was a paranormal researcher, and she’d been haunted enough times at Skully Manor to know for herself that ghosts were real.

“I’m not *afraid* of ghosts,” Lilac corrected herself. She walked slowly to the table and sat down on the tasseled stool. Referencing the open book, she read out loud.

“Light the candles and burn some sage,” she said this extra slow to try to keep her voice from shaking, but her voice still quavered.

She lit a match off of the candle that was already burning and set the other four candles aflame. She unscrewed the lid from the ancient jar of dried sage. She took one of the leaves out and crushed it up over a candle. Then she read the next step from the book.

“Circle your table three times, clockwise, imagining a circle of white light forming and protecting you from harm.” She stood up and circled the table three times, trying to imagine a white light. She wasn’t sure if she’d done it right. She sat back down.

She skimmed the book again and began to read in a trembling whisper.

“Summon the spirits to join you in a clear, loud voice.” Her whole body shook. She took a deep breath and set her hands down purposefully on the table. She closed her eyes.

"I..." she squeaked. Phlegm caught in her throat and squelched any sound that might have come out. A mighty roar of thunder struck suddenly outside.

Lilac's arms flailed up, instinctively, as she clamored to the floor and huddled under the table. She realized it was just lightning and got back up. She sat down on the stool, the tassels swaying wildly from side to side. Lilac slammed her palms down on the table and stood back up.

"I call upon the spirits that reside here!" she yelled suddenly, as loudly as she could.

A powerful electric feeling came over her. It felt strange and somewhat scary, but in this sense, she found the voice to carry on.

"I call upon you!" she said even louder, raising her arms into the air dramatically, a move she would have never expected herself to make, but she did.

"To join me!" she continued. She paused.

"Can you hear me?" she yelled. "Make yourself known!"

Thunder struck again, and Lilac jumped at a terrible clang and bang coming from the library on the far side of Skully Manor. Then something caught her eye upstairs. The sconce lights in the Hall of the Little Girl Ghost began to flicker.

"I COMMAND YOU TO LEAVE!" Lilac roared, so loud that she felt her throat start to burn a little.

Thunder rumbled again, and there was another loud clatter and bang from the library.

Bam. Bam. Bam.

It was a sound Lilac recognized. She tried to pretend it wasn't, but it was. It was Mr. Fright.

Lilac didn't say anything else. She put her arms down, abruptly, when she realized she was still holding them up in the air.

Tink. She heard a faint sound upstairs. *Tink, tink.* Her blood sank to an icy cold. She recognized that sound, too.

It was the ghost nickamed "Jack." A little boy poltergeist who was known for appearing with jacks, bats, rubber balls, candy, and other small objects. According to legend, he was the younger brother of the Little Girl Ghost. According to Lilac, he was the one who played all sorts of terrible tricks on her, keeping her awake and terrorizing her all night—until she refused to sleep in her bedroom anymore.

Tink, tink, tink. Lilac heard the sound growing closer. The landing of the second floor began to glow with a ghastly tone, and there stood little Jack behind the banister, in a pale blue sailor suit and cap, a rubber ball and bat under his arm, the mischievous grin on his face.

"Ahem," Lilac heard a polite cough from upstairs. Before she had time to panic and run, another figure appeared. As if this could not get any worse, there stood the Butler. She had only seen him a handful of times. One of these times, he appeared with his severed head on a platter, right in front of Lilac and the tutor that used to come to the house. Lilac thought the Butler was horrifying. And the tutor never came back. Lilac felt a shiver.

The lights flickered brightly in the upstairs hall. Then, one by one, the lights down the corridor turned on by themselves. The pendant lamp illuminated, even though Lilac knew the bulb had burnt out years ago. Lilac felt another chill creep through the manor, and the familiar sweet and musty scent of ghosts grew even stronger. The chandelier in the center of the foyer began to glow with a dim light. Lilac's shiver became a visible tremor that she could not control.

At that moment, the apparition of the Little Girl Ghost appeared just on the other side of Lilac's séance table. Pale blue and eerily translucent—yet clear as day—the light of Lilac's candles illuminated right through the ghost.

Lilac took a deep breath and stared into the grim face of the Little Girl Ghost. She had sunken, sad eyes, pupils like darkly twisted galaxies. The ghost looked as if she had died quite young, perhaps only a year or two younger than Lilac was now. She wore a forlorn look on her face. Her hair was light brown, and half of it was pulled up on top of her head and tied with a droopy, sad-looking blue bow. She wore a ribboned, pleated party dress with a ruffly collar that was buttoned all the way up her neck. On her feet were shiny patent leather shoes with fancy socks, not unlike something Lilac would have liked to wear if she had ever received a party invitation.

Trembling, mouth agape, unable to hide her utter panic which would have been visible to anyone nearby, Lilac stuttered to herself.

"Tell them to leave the house!" Lilac said under her breath, "Tell them to leave!"

Lilac tried to command the three ghosts to leave but just stammered and shook so much that she felt herself buckling at the knees despite her intention to act and speak powerfully.

"I'm... Milly," the ghost said softly to Lilac Skully.

Lilac could not stand any longer and fell backward onto the tasseled stool, which tipped over, dumping her onto the floor.

"Liiiiiii-lac?" Milly wailed and started to float closer.

"N... no!!" Lilac gasped and stammered.

Milly stopped, and the sad look on her face grew

even longer.

"Why are you afraid of me?" the ghost said to Lilac Skully.

Lilac could think of all sorts of reasons. The way her voice wailed and cried through the night, for one. The sounds of her little shoes stepping slowly down the hall. The heart-wrenching look in her eyes that Lilac had awoke to many times when she still slept in her bedroom.

But then, Lilac saw something strange. Ghostly tears began to fall down Milly's face, then bounced off of her cheeks and disappeared into clouds of fine dust as they hit the ground.

"I'm just a little girl!" cried the Little Girl Ghost in despair.

"I..." Lilac didn't quite know what to say. "You're a ghost!" she blurted out from the floor, sitting back on her hands. Milly began to wail and cry even more.

"I can't... help... it!" Milly sobbed and sat herself down on her knees a few feet away from Lilac.

"No one... understands me!" Milly cried. Her apparition began to fade away as she whimpered.

"W... Wait!!" Lilac called out, and sat forwards towards the ghost, "Milly, it's okay!"

Milly's apparition popped back to full form instantly, and she caught Lilac's gaze again square in the eye.

Lilac was taken aback again, as she looked deep into the swirling dark eyes of the ghost, but tried not to flinch or show that she was terribly afraid.

Lilac continued softly, "I mean... I might understand how you feel," she said to Milly.

She had felt eerily cold up to this point, but her cheeks and neck started to feel quite warm. A lump formed in her throat, and her face became wet with tears. Lilac choked out the words, "Everyone is afraid of me, too."

It was true for the most part. Not quite everyone, but almost. In Lilac's short nine-and-three-quarters years of being a Skully, she'd been on the receiving end of more than her fair share of bullying and drama. She was the weirdo, the freak, the girl from the haunted house. The strange daughter of the even stranger Paranormal Researcher Dr. Skully. The girl whose mother had died under odd circumstances when Lilac was still quite small. She was that girl. The one that couldn't have friends over to play because her house was haunted, and anyone who came to visit left quickly, most of them running away in horror.

Yes, Lilac Skully understood what it was like to be misunderstood, even though she was *just* a little girl.

5.

Paranormal Activity

Milly blinked and stopped crying, her head tilted in a momentary state of shock, mouth agape. She looked at Lilac. Lilac looked back at her, her head tilted the other direction, with a similar look of shock on her face. Lilac heard a *tap, tap, tap,* and glanced up at the second floor landing. Milly's brother was bouncing his rubber ball. And the Butler was still there too, trying to stay out of their conversation with his hands clasped behind his back. Lilac looked back at Milly. Both of the girls stared at each other and tried to figure out what they should do or say next.

"Thanks, Lilac," Milly said finally, "I guess that does make me feel a little bit better."

Lilac smiled a bit and sat up, crossing her legs. She continued to look at Milly curiously and tilted her head the other direction.

The chilling ice between them had been broken, and Lilac suddenly wanted to know so much more about Milly. What did it feel like to be a ghost? Where do ghosts go when they disappear? Could a ghost pick her up and help her fly through the air?

But the curiosities were interrupted by the sound of shattering glass in the library. The banging and clattering that started during the séance was getting louder and more frequent.

"Oh dear," the voice of the Butler muttered from the landing on the second floor. "It seems Mr. Fright is upset."

"He's certainly not happy." Milly added.

Lilac knew who Mr. Fright was, and he was never happy. His claim to fame was that he was a particularly angry poltergeist. And worse, he hated little girls.

"He heard what you said," Milly said to Lilac in a bit of a scolding tone.

"What?" Lilac asked, "What did I say?"

"You said, 'I command you to leeeaave!'" the Little Girl Ghost imitated Lilac, raising her arms up in the air.

"I... I said that..." Lilac admitted oh so quietly, all of a sudden wishing she hadn't.

Bam. Crash. Thud. The door to the library was hit with an object that was thrown from inside. Lilac jumped.

"He didn't like that at all." Milly continued, shaking her head enough that bits of iridescent dust shimmied down around her.

"We've haunted here for over one hundred years, you know," she added matter-of-factly.

Bam. Lilac heard another noise, this time even closer. She stood up and took a few steps back. Mr. Fright was on the other side of the door, she reckoned, just a few feet away.

"Well, you can't leave now," said Milly. "You called us to join you." She raised her eyes and waved her arm out to the inviting table and atmosphere that Lilac had set up.

Bam. Bam. Bam. Mr. Fright was banging on the door on the other side of the foyer. The handle of the door shook and rattled as he tried to open it. Lilac stepped back again.

"It's too laaaate, Liiii-lac," Milly said, shaking her head again.

The handle of the door started to jiggle at an unnatural frequency. One screw fell out, then another. Then the heavy iron doorknob popped off and fell with a clunk to the floor.

There was an unnervingly long moment of silence.

Bang. Someone kicked the door, and it flung open. Lilac looked into the darkness of the doorway, unable to breathe.

"Mr. Fright, please. There's no reason to overreact," the rational voice of the Butler called down from upstairs.

Then Lilac heard one footstep, then another. She

followed the sound of leather boots ambling towards her, step by step. But there was no figure or apparition to go with it. One more step, then two. The sweet musty smell of ghosts began to envelop her, and she started to feel so dizzy she thought she might faint.

Then, the apparition of Mr. Fright materialized.

He had dirty blonde hair with a deep, wide-set part in the middle, the two sides sticking up, almost like horns. He had a thin, misshapen nose, a patchy mustache, and seedy, glaring eyes that pierced Lilac Skully's soul when she caught his glance.

Before Mr. Fright could tell her that there was no way he was leaving, especially not on account of a little girl, she turned and ran.

She ran back through the dining hall and into the kitchen, her fingers shaking dreadfully as she did up the locks and latches on the door. She flung herself into the window seat, tore off her fancy velvet hat, and buried her head in the cushions. She could still hear Mr. Fright screaming, banging, and clattering out in the main hall. *Screech. Bang. Thwap.*

She held two pillows tight over her ears in a failed attempt to drown out the sounds of the poltergeist.

Then she heard something else.

"Liiii-lac!" The familiar voice wailed. She looked up

to see Milly floating just through the kitchen door.

"Get out of here!" Lilac jumped up and screamed at Milly. "This is my kitchen! This room is mine!"

She picked up the nearest book, *Charlotte's Web*, and threw it at the Little Girl Ghost. Milly's apparition disappeared instantly, but her voice did not. It came even closer to Lilac's left ear and spoke again.

"Fire!" she wailed. "Lilac! The candles!"

Lilac's eyes grew wide as she heard more banging, yelling, and now the worst kind of disembodied laughing and chuckling from the hall of Skully Manor.

She ran to the pantry without hesitation and grabbed the rusty old fire extinguisher. She unlocked the kitchen doors as quickly as she could and charged through the dining room and into the foyer, the nozzle of the large fire extinguisher poised and ready in front of her.

By the time she got to the blaze, it had taken up both of the antique tablecloths. It was lucky for Lilac that the table was made of metal and marble. She jiggled the pin on the fire extinguisher several times to get it to budge.

Mr. Fright swooped in and picked up the burning tablecloths, lifting them up into the air as he cackled and swirled around, flying the flaming fabric through the foyer of Skully Manor.

Lilac got the pin out and pulled the trigger of the

fire extinguisher, the force of it blowing her backward, a great cloud of white dust shooting wildly up into the air. Mr. Fright wailed with laughter and swooped the burning tablecloths down over Lilac. The heat of the flames was so intense, she was forced to the ground and flung herself away from the fire on her hands and knees. Mr. Fright swooped back up and dropped the flames over the open doors to the library. The fire crackled louder and intensified as it got a hold on the wooden doors. Great plumes of gray smoke began to rise.

Lilac had no time to panic. She picked up the fire extinguisher again and aimed the nozzle at the fire, the powder spraying wildly as she struggled to get control.

She felt an unnerving, otherworldly, and violent push on her back. Mr. Fright had shoved her from behind in a cheap shot, and she was flung forward to the ground, the wind knocked out of her. She wrestled the fire extinguisher back into her arms, knowing she did not have time to waste or stand back up or breathe. She pulled the trigger on the fire extinguisher once more, grappling with the nozzle with every fiber of her body, and aiming the powder up at the fire.

Bang. She heard the loudest bang of the night, so close behind her, she felt her teeth chatter in her head and a bell ringing in her ears.

Mr. Fright had knocked the old and grotesque crest

of the House of Skully down from the wall. The Crest of the House of Skully was rumored to have a real human skull and bones on it. It was the first thing you saw hanging over the foyer when you walked into Skully Manor, and Lilac had always hated it. She hated it more now that it had almost fallen on her and killed her. Mr. Fright was cackling loudly, satisfied with his work, and floated upwards, looking around for more things to throw at Lilac.

With the fire and candles out, Lilac did not leave time for Mr. Fright's next attack. She spun around and ran back to the kitchen as fast as she could, slamming the door shut. She locked the locks, sprung into her window seat and pulled the blankets over her.

Bam. Bam. Bam. She heard the sound through the pillows over her ears, as Mr. Fright continued his haunting.

By morning, Lilac was exhausted and cold and had not slept at all. Mr. Fright had been yelling and rattling the large clanking doors of Skully Manor all night.

But it was not just the poltergeist that had kept Lilac up. It was also the anxious thoughts running through her mind.

With her father gone for so long, Lilac feared that she'd be found out as an unsupervised or neglected child, and she'd be sent to a foster home, or an orphanage, to live with strangers whom she did not know. For a split second, the three terrifying months she had spent at the boarding school flashed through her mind. She buried the memory again deeply, as fast as she could. Instead, she thought about the books she'd read that said what happened to children in this kind of situation, and it wasn't good. She shuddered.

She'd been trying to squelch this worry and not think about it. But after last night's events, it crept up and plagued her over and over as she lay in bed, listening to the sounds of Mr. Fright rattling into the night.

The terrible thought that Mr. Fright was being too loud began to overwhelm Lilac as the sun rose next morning, and he still hadn't stopped haunting. What if she was found out? The last thing she wanted was for any kind of attention to be drawn to her, a little girl living alone at Skully Manor.

6.

News You Can Use

Knock, knock, knock! Lilac sprung up out of bed and then froze. Someone was knocking right there on the kitchen door. The sun was still dim and just starting to rise.

Casper disappeared under the china cabinet, and Lilac crouched down onto the floor, careful to stay out of sight should any curtains be open a crack.

"Hello?" She heard a muffled man's voice call from outside. "Mr. Skully?" the voice called out, obviously annoyed. "Anyone home?" The man walked to another window in the back of the house and knocked again. "What's going on in there? What's that banging noise?" the man's voice called. "It's been going on all night! Jiminy Christmas!"

Lilac was on her hands and knees, still crouched down in the maid's quarters. She thought she recognized the voice, their neighbor, Mr. Jones. He was exactly the sort of person that Lilac didn't want knowing she was home alone. He would turn her in, she was sure of it.

"You're attracting a bit of a crowd out here,"

Lilac heard him call out again. "And driving down the property values, this place is falling apart," he said as he started to walk away.

Crunch, crunch, crunch. He walked back up the gravel drive on the side of the house.

Creak. Clink. Lilac heard Mr. Jones shut the gate behind him as he left her yard.

Bam. Bam. Bam. She heard Mr. Fright rattle the doors to the basement again.

"I wonder what he meant, attracting a crowd?" Lilac wondered. She put the tea kettle on the stove and set out her teacup. She set out a small bite of food for Casper, who ate it all at once.

She went to the farthest kitchen window that had a view of the front of the house and peered out to the street. Mr. Jones was talking to two men who had just got out of a small, rusty blue car. Mr. Jones waved his arms around like he was exasperated, and shook his head. The two men seemed to be ignoring him and were pointing towards her house and unloading various pieces of electrical equipment with antennas and cameras, setting them up on the side of the road.

Bam. Bam. Bam. Mr. Fright rattled the front door of Skully Manor. The two men outside jumped to attention, one of them raised his glasses and pulled a handheld recorder out of his pocket.

The men started to walk closer, but Mr. Jones motioned to them as if to stay back.

Bam. Bam. Bam! Mr. Fright went off again, loud enough to be heard outside. The lights in the house flickered, and the streetlights outside flickered with them. Lilac heard an excited hoot from the men at the front of her house, and their voices grew louder.

Lilac continued to watch them. Mr. Jones walked back towards his house, still shaking his head. Then Lilac's teakettle began to whistle. She ran to silence it, knowing that the whistle could have blown her cover. She poured her cup of tea and went back to the window. She sat up on the counter cross-legged and looked back outside.

Another man and a woman walked up to the blue car. Lilac sat up straighter. She looked harder.

"I know them!" she whispered loudly to herself. "The Mulligans! He's the man that got scratched and ran screaming."

She stared out the window and held her breath. They were local ghost investigators, and acquaintances of her father. She sipped her tea.

A few years back, her father allowed amateur researchers to come into Skully Manor for paranormal investigations. The couple had been inside the house before, but on that occasion, they didn't make it more than fifteen or twenty minutes in the basement with Mr. Fright before the man ran out with scratches on his back, followed by his wife and their equipment.

Lilac remembered feeling a pang of envy as she watched them drive off that day. They could run away from the ghosts. They didn't have to stay. But Skully Manor was Lilac's home. And there was nowhere else for her to go.

Before she could feel too sorry for herself—the girl who lived in the haunted house—someone else walked up to the little crowd that was gathering in front of Skully Manor. This time, it was a woman in a blue business suit, holding a large foam-tipped microphone.

"Oh no!" Lilac whispered to herself in horror, setting her teacup down so she could clutch her forehead and process what she'd seen. "It's the local news!"

Bam. Bam. Bam! Mr. Fright rattled the front doors, loud enough to get a big reaction and another cheer from the ghost investigators outside, ready with their recorders, receivers, antennas and various instruments. The lady from the news broke from the pack and walked out of Lilac's view.

Lilac jumped off the counter and ran back to her maid's quarters. She turned on the small TV and found the news channel, KPBJ on channel six, which was on a commercial break. She turned the volume as low as she could and put a blanket over herself and the TV to dim the light, just in case anyone was snooping around the back of the house again.

The commercials ended and a man in the local morning newsroom appeared on TV.

"Well, we're back! And we've got some excitement to report... a little ghost-action out in Steamville this morning!" The man in the newsroom chuckled and shuffled his note cards on the table. "Oooooh-Ooooooooooh!!" he mocked and laughed again, waving his fingers and wailing like a ghost.

Lilac rolled her eyes.

"Maryellen!" he said. "Isn't it a little early for Halloween?"

Before Lilac could answer that ridiculous question, as it was already October, she got a bit of a shock when her house appeared live, right in front of her on TV.

"Oh no!" Lilac gasped.

"Well you might think so, Steve." said Maryellen with a big, big, smile and wide doe eyes. "But apparently it's always Halloween here at Skully Manor, one of the area's most notorious haunted houses."

Lilac slapped her forehead and groaned.

Maryellen continued without a pause. "Skully Manor is famous for hosting a wide range of paranormal activity throughout this past century. And calls have been flooding into the local police and news stations since last night when it's believed that one of the poltergeists inside has suddenly become active."

"Oh no!" Lilac gasped again at the thought of concerned calls flooding the police, alerting them to her unsupervised existence.

"I'm here with amateur ghost hunter, Bobby Joe Mulligan," the camera panned out a bit, showing Maryellen standing next to the man Lilac recognized—the man who ran screaming in fright from Skully Manor.

"Bobby Joe," she continued in a sensational newsy tone, "Can you tell us what might be happening inside Skully Manor? We've been hearing some loud banging noises, the lights up and down the block have been flickering, we've heard several reports of vertigo, and there's definitely a weird feeling here, almost like a dizzy, lightheaded feeling. I've witnessed it. You've witnessed it. What is going on here?"

"Thanks, Maryellen!" Bobby Joe responded, "Well, my wife and I have been researching local ghosts including the ones here at Skully Manor for seven years now," he told the camera enthusiastically, "and I think what we're witnessing today is an outburst of poltergeist activity, possibly the notorious ghost, Frederick Wright, who's more commonly known as Mr. Fright."

Maryellen's body recoiled backwards as you might when you are afraid, but the big, TV smile on her face did not fade.

Bam. Bam. Bam. Lilac heard the sounds again in her house, the lights dimmed, and she felt a twinge of the low, almost nauseating pulse that often went with his more provoked hauntings. She watched the people on TV react to what was going on.

"Wow!" Maryellen said to the camera, steadying herself a little. "Did you feel that?" she said to Bobby Joe, who nodded, seriously. "Did you hear that?" she said to the television audience back at home.

She turned back to Bobby Joe. "Can we get a bit closer and see if we can get some audio on the camera? Knock on the door and see if anyone is home?"

Lilac froze. Oh no. No. Horror overcame her as she watched the discussion in front of her house live on TV.

"I wouldn't recommend it," Bobby Joe said very solemnly and suddenly.

"Phew." Lilac said quietly.

"While there are some paranormal energy fields we can attempt to pick up with our equipment from outside, we give the Skully family their space out of mutual respect..." Bobby Joe said and nodded, "I've worked with Mr. Skully—Dr. Skully—I should say, as he's a notable paranormal researcher. He's been kind enough to let us in for our investigations a few times, but..." Bobby Joe started to get visibly flustered. His arms folded, and he was tripping on his words. Lilac just wanted him to stop talking about her family and her house and for everyone to go away.

"Stop talking! Stop talking!" she whispered and tried to will him to stop with her mind.

Maryellen's interest piqued. "Ah! So you've actually been inside *Skully Manor*! And people are living there? Tell us, did you see any ghosts? Did you record any evidence of their existence?" She held the microphone back up to Bobby Joe Mulligan's mouth.

"Well," Bobby Joe stammered enthusiastically, "Yes, I've recorded some audio that we believe to be the voice of Frederick Wright," He held his tape recorder up to the microphone and pressed play. A low-quality recorded cackle played through the speaker.

"That's Mr. Fright, all right," Lilac said under her breath.

"Wow!" Maryellen exclaimed excitedly for the camera.

Bobby Joe continued seriously, "But you've got to understand some of the ghosts you're dealing with here are pretty scary, I'd even say dangerous wh..."

"Dangerous?!" Maryellen interrupted, her enthusiasm intensified by the prospect of danger.

"Well, yes, when it's a poltergeist who, you know," Bobby Joe motioned with his hands, "might be able to throw or move objects around... I was even scratched, see?" He pulled out a worn photo from his pocket, where you could see three terrible red scratches across his back. Lilac felt a chill, and all the hair stood up on her arms. She knew the scratches were real, and Mr. Fright had caused them.

Bam. Bam. Bam. Mr. Fright rattled the great front doors of Skully Manor. Lilac curled up and tried to become invisible.

"Stop! Mr. Fright, stop!" she said, hoping to will him to stop. But he did not stop.

Bam. Bam. Bam. She heard again as the lights flickered and electricity pulsed. She heard more gasps outside her house.

On TV, Maryellen reacted with joy, her huge smile even bigger.

"Whoa! Did you hear that!" she exclaimed and held the microphone out to Bobby Joe's mouth again. "I'm certainly feeling something here, whew!" She fanned herself with her free hand.

But Bobby Joe did not respond. He held out a receiver with an antenna and put on his headphones, in an attempt to capture some of the paranormal activity. He fiddled with knobs on his equipment and focused intently.

"I'm attempting to pick up evidence of the poltergeist!" Bobby Joe responded quite loud, his voice both muffled by his headphones and amplified by his excitement.

"Can we get closer?" Maryellen asked again.

"Dr. Skully has asked for privacy for the sake of his young daughter!" Bobby Joe replied without hesitation. "But he has allowed us to continue research from a respectable distance!"

"His daughter?" Maryellen picked up. "A little girl? Is there a little girl living in this haunted house?" She held the microphone back to his mouth.

"Yes!" he replied, loudly. Lilac felt a sense of impending doom. The last thing she wanted was for anyone to know she existed.

The TV camera zoomed in on Maryellen.

"And there you have it, folks. We've confirmed poltergeist activity is going on here at Skully Manor, where a little girl inside may be in danger." Maryellen gave the camera a wide-eyed stare. "And it looks like the Steamville Police have just pulled up to the home and are about to knock on the door... And now to a commercial break."

Lilac began to panic. She shut off the TV, not because

the commercials were twice as loud as the news, but because she could not believe what was happening.

Bam. Bam. Bam. She heard again from the hall as the light flickered.

"The police are here!" she gasped to herself, falling to the floor and lying face up, staring at the ceiling and feeling her world collapse around her, wondering what she could do to stop this from happening.

"I'll be found out!" she gasped. All the terrible things she'd read about children who were placed under the care of guardians ran through her head. "I've got to make him stop!" She panicked.

Lilac's shaky fingers tied double knots as she put on her sneakers. She put on her hooded rain jacket and grabbed her amulet and lilac sachet.

She unlocked the doors to the dining hall and took a deep breath.

7.
Hiding in Plain Sight

Knock, knock, knock! Lilac would have jumped out of her sneakers if she hadn't tied them on so tightly. Someone was rapping loudly at her back kitchen door. Lilac fell to the floor and slithered behind a cabinet, out of sight from any windows.

"Steamville Police!" a woman's voice called out.

Knock, knock, knock! The police pounded again on the back kitchen door. They were too close.

Thump, thump, thump. That was the sound of Lilac's heart. She heard the officer's footsteps crunching slowly in the gravel outside. She peeked around the corner of the cabinet and realized she'd left the curtain open.

The window was about as high up as an adult's head, and the officer was moving in that direction. Lilac darted out as quick and as low as she could. She jumped up and tugged the curtain shut, just as the officer rounded the corner. The officer must have sensed Lilac's movement.

"Hello?" she called out again and rapped on the same window. Anyone home? Everything ok in there? Steamville Police here. Do you need any help?"

Lilac plastered herself to the floor. She stayed silent for a moment and then heard the footsteps start up again towards the front of the house.

As fast but as quietly as she could, she charged through the doors and into the dining hall. Out of the corner of her eye, she saw the silhouette of the officer walking outside towards another open blind that she'd left open about a week ago, thinking her father's car had returned. She couldn't get to the window in time to close the blind. So she flung herself forward towards the gigantic carved dining table, and crouched down behind one of the thick table legs. She did not breathe. She pretended she was invisible.

The officer bent down and peeked in the window through the open blind, her hands cupped to the sides of her eyes to get a good look inside.

After a pause she felt would never end, Lilac heard the officer's footsteps continue again towards the front of the house. Lilac let out a wavering breath and continued to run through the foyer and up the stairs.

Bam. Bam. Bam. Rattle. Mr. Fright shook the doors as Lilac passed.

Lilac ran down the Hall of the Little Girl Ghost, tears welling up in her eyes as she imagined life in foster care, possibly a group home where she was forced to play team sports. Her lower lip trembled. She wiped her eyes and turned the corner into the hall.

"Milly!" she called in a loud whisper, hoping the ghost would hear her. "I need your help!" She couldn't stop her voice from shaking. "Milly!" Lilac continued down the hall, choking on her words, but did not see Milly. She looked into her bedroom, the one she never used, and was taken aback.

There were three ghosts in her room.

One was the elusive form of the Butler, whose apparition disappeared as soon as Lilac came to the doorway. The second was the creepy boy in the sailor suit, Milly's little brother. He was sitting in the rocking chair in the corner of Lilac's room, slowly rocking back and forth. Lilac would have run at the sight of either of these ghosts, but the third ghost in her room was the one Lilac was trying to find. It was Milly.

"I need your help," Lilac said again, unable to hide the trembling in her voice and body.

Milly started to float up slowly, a worried gaze in her eyes. "It's worse than you think!" she said to Lilac.

Lilac's heart fell from her throat to the pit of her stomach. Worse? How could this be any worse? She didn't want to know. But she waited anxiously for Milly to elaborate.

"We're in danger," Milly finally gave more information after a dramatic pause. "There's someone outside..." She gave a tragic stare out towards the front of the house.

"I know!" Lilac replied, exasperated. "It's the police! And you've got to make Mr. Fright stop drawing attention!"

"No!" Milly wailed, "Not them! Worse! And you won't hear another peep from Mr. Fright." she added and sighed, her apparition flickering and fading out slightly as if she could not carry on.

"We're in danger, Lilac!" she cried out again, "Graaave danger!" the ghost added, intensely, possibly just for emphasis, maybe because she was truly that frightened.

"Wh... what do you mean?" Lilac felt her heart pounding faster. "Why are you in danger? And how will you make Mr. Fright stop? He's been banging around for hours!"

"The ghost-nappers are back," Milly spoke these words ever so softly. "The ones that took the Blue Lady." Her voice wailed and drew out as she lifted one hand and rose up further, floating across the room. "Their van is parked just outside." Her ghostly finger extended and pointed.

For a brief moment, Lilac felt as if she could feel what Milly was feeling. She felt lost and hopelessly misunderstood. Afraid that if she showed the world who she truly was, she'd be shunned.

"They took the Blue Lady?" Lilac asked, trying to wrap her mind around what Milly was saying. Milly nodded.

Lilac had heard of the Blue Lady. She was the one apparition of Skully Manor that Lilac had never seen for herself, and Lilac was perfectly happy with that. Because legend had it that if you became entranced by the hypnotic dancing of the beautiful Blue Lady and followed her through the woods, you'd wander and die. You'd become a lost soul—haunting the woods at night for all eternity.

Lilac thought for a moment and remembered a frightening incident that had taken place outside of Skully Manor in the back garden. It had been at least a year ago, maybe two. She heard terrible noises outside the window and had frozen in panic. Her father wouldn't tell her what had happened, other than someone took something of value from the garden. He seemed upset, she recalled. Distraught, even. Lilac wondered if the thing of value had been the Blue Lady. She fought off a shiver.

"How do you *take* a ghost?" Lilac asked.

The little girl ghost locked her gaze with Lilac's. She narrowed her eyes and suddenly looked very angry.

"They sucked her up in that horrible... orb!"

"It was horrible!" the boy ghost in the sailor suit yelled out as he flew from the rocking chair, nearly knocking it over. He landed back on Lilac's bed with a cloud of dust and pulled a teddy bear over his head. "And they're back!"

"Archie!" Milly yelled in a loud whisper, shushing the boy. "We've all got to be very quiet!" Archie's apparition faded suddenly, and the teddy bear plopped down to the floor.

Lilac realized that Mr. Fright's banging noises had stopped. But she still heard the knocking on the door downstairs.

Knock, knock, knock. It was the police again, this time using the large iron skull-shaped knocker on the front door of Skully Manor.

"Steamville Police!" Lilac heard from downstairs.

"The police are still here!" Lilac whispered to Milly. "We've got to get them to leave!" she tried to explain.

"Why are you afraid of the police?" Milly asked gently.

"I don't want them to find me," Lilac responded. "My father's not here, and children aren't supposed to be left alone this long, I don't think."

"I see," Milly said, nodding her head in sympathy. "Let's just sit here and be very quiet, then."

Bleep, bleep, beep! They heard the sound of the

police radio coming from just downstairs below Lilac's bedroom windows.

"Officer Grimble to headquarters, come in. This is Officer Grimble at the old Skully Manor."

Bleep, beep, beep!

"Come in, Officer Grimble!" said a muffled voice through the radio.

Bleep, bleep, bleep!

"We may need some further investigation of what's going on here, make sure everyone's alright. If you could send..."

"No!" Lilac mouthed silently to Milly.

Screech! bleep! Squee-bleep! Screech! Lilac heard the radio sputter static and beep oddly a few times.

The officer was interrupted.

Milly squeezed her dark swirling eyes shut. She stuck her arms out, slightly bent, her fingers and neck stiff at odd, contorted angles.

"No!" the static voice on the radio said suddenly. "We've got an all-points bulletin emergency over at 34th and Romany. We need all officers on the scene, and that includes you, Grimble. All officers on the scene, I repeat. Over and out."

Lilac looked in amazement at Milly, who was mouthing the words that were coming out of the police radio outside.

Beeep! Bleep!

"But..." Officer Grimble tried to respond into the radio.

"No further investigation needed at Skully Manor. That's an order from the Chief. Over and out!" Milly's words came through the voice on the radio again.

The girls sat together in silence on Lilac's bed, the bed Lilac had not slept in for several years. They listened. They heard footsteps on the old wooden porch downstairs as the officer started walking away. One. Two Three. Four. Five wooden steps.

"Ok, nothing to see here, folks!" the voice of Office Grimble called to the people gathered outside. "Let's clear out here, ok? There are no ghosts."

And a moment later, they heard police sirens blare as Officer Grimble sped away.

8.

Strange Friends

"How did you..." Lilac asked Milly in astonishment. She didn't need to finish her question for Milly to understand what she wanted to ask.

"One of the benefits of being a ghost, I guess," Milly responded, breaking into a slight smile, the first hint of a smile that Lilac had seen from the Little Girl Ghost.

"I can do things with radio frequencies." Milly shrugged. "My brother and I listen in on the police radio all the time." Milly swung her legs up on Lilac's bed with a gentle poof of ghostly dust, and lay back, leaning against the headboard.

Lilac did the same and sat side by side with Milly. She felt a little taken aback that Milly had made herself so very comfortable and at home in what had been her bedroom. But she didn't make an issue of it or mention it.

Lilac fixed her eyes on the translucent pale blue, scuffed, patent leather party shoes and delicate ruffly white socks that Milly had haunted in for the past one hundred years. She thought about how different they seemed now compared to the other night in the storm. They had looked terrifying then, but now, they just looked kind of sad. The silence became overwhelming, yet Lilac didn't know what to say next.

"What now?" Lilac asked Milly, a few moments later.

"I guess we need to stay quiet and hope they leave!" Milly said.

They sat in silence for what seemed like hours but may have only been minutes.

"So they kidnapped the Blue Lady?" Lilac asked.

"Yes," Milly replied with a hush.

"In a... horrible... orb?" Lilac asked, not exactly sure what that was.

Milly sighed and hesitantly replied, "Yes, in that most horrible orb." She then closed her eyes and set her head back against the headboard. She shuddered.

"I don't know how long ago it was," Milly went on to tell Lilac. "Time kind of does funny things when you're a ghost." She stopped for a bit, and Lilac did not push for more answers.

"She was the lady ghost that haunted the garden and danced in the woods," Milly clarified, although Lilac already knew that.

"She was beautiful." Milly lamented, gazing out into nothingness. "Her hair. Her dress. Her smile." She drew these statements out dramatically. "She kind of looked after us here, like a guardian, I guess," Milly added eventually. "She's haunted for much longer than most ghosts." Milly trailed off in sad, silent memory.

"I think I remember when she was... taken," Lilac said, trying to recall more details from the frightening incident that had happened outside her window.

"My father told me something was stolen from the garden." Lilac wracked her brain but could not come up with the details. "He wouldn't tell me exactly what it was," Lilac added. "And he wouldn't call the police, I thought he definitely should..." she trailed off a bit.

"Your father seems kind enough," Milly said hesitantly and then added, "A bit strange."

Lilac sighed. She knew.

Creak. Creak. Creak. A familiar sound returned.

Archie rocked slowly in Lilac's rocking chair, staring at her with wide, empty dark eyes. When she used to sleep in this bedroom, he'd woken her up in the middle of the night—countless times—in just this same creepy way. Lilac looked away and shuddered, although she felt a bit sad that he must have been an adorable boy when he was living—dusty blonde hair, rosy cheeks, and his Sunday best--a classic sailor suit, knee socks, and saddle shoes.

"Oh, don't mind him," Milly said, noting Lilac's discomfort. "That's just my little brother, Archie."

Lilac could have written a book filled with horrifying tales of being chased, taunted, and tormented all over the manor by that same little ghost. He was particularly good at popping out at the most unexpected times, frightening Lilac just as she thought she was safe or alone. Milly tried to smooth it over further.

"He likes you," she said to convince Lilac. "He's just funny that way." Lilac looked back at her but didn't respond.

She remembered all of the times she'd heard his jacks and rubber ball in the hallway. *Plop. Tink. Tink. Tink.* She'd hear coming from the darkness. Then she'd realize she was trapped with nowhere to go. He'd peer his head around the doorway, slowly, a wild, childish grin on his face. Lilac tried to remember if it was an incident with Archie that had finally scared her out of her bedroom for good. She was fairly certain it was.

"He was the one that kept you from falling off the roof the other night," Milly explained, trying to come up with more reasons to show Lilac that she needn't be afraid of Archie.

"What?" Lilac said. "When I almost fell off the roof? There was someone who helped me?"

Milly nodded. "None of us want to hurt you," she

said. "Well, except for Mr. Fright," she sighed. "Archie just likes to play games, and you know," Milly bobbed her head side to side a little, "I think he wants to be friends," she hinted to Lilac. "It gets boring, haunting the same place for so long."

Lilac laughed a little. Then she got more serious and asked, "Can't you leave and... go places?"

"No," Milly stuttered a little. "Some ghosts can, but... " She stopped. "Most of us here at the manor can't walk and wander." Milly looked aside pensively. "But the Blue Lady could wander anywhere she liked..." she added.

Lilac wasn't familiar with the term "walk and wander," but she guessed it meant that Milly was sort of trapped there in Skully Manor. She didn't press it further.

"It depends on what kind of ghost," Milly offered. "And you know," she nodded to Lilac and narrowed her dark swirling eyes. "It depends on the circumstances."

"The circumstances?" Lilac asked, confused.

Milly sighed. "Yes, the circumstances."

Lilac looked back at her blankly.

Milly then added loudly, "Of your death!" She waved her hand up in the air, as if it was so obvious, and crossed her arms in front of her.

Lilac didn't ask any other questions that might be

too personal for ghosts. Their deaths might be sensitive subjects. Of course they were, she realized, and felt slightly embarrassed.

They spent several hours in each others company, a lot of silence in between curious bits of conversation as they wondered more about each other.

"Where'd Archie... go?" Lilac tried to ask when she realized that Archie had silently disappeared from the room at some point.

"Hard to explain if you're not dead," Milly said after a pause. "But I guess it's sort of like that moment just before you fall asleep, where for a second, you don't really know if you're dreaming or not."

Lilac knew exactly how that felt. Not so bad actually, she thought. She kind of enjoyed those funny moments in-between consciousness.

"And then you just stay there the whole time? Where does the..." Lilac waved her arms around a little. "... *ghost* part of you go?" she asked.

"Oh we're still here, but it takes energy to appear," Milly said plainly. "Sometimes lots depending on what you do,"

"So where's Archie?" Lilac asked, still trying to figure out how it all worked.

"He could be anywhere in the house or garden,

but probably in one of the rooms on the third floor," Milly said. "No one ever goes up there, so he likes to use the space to play," she explained to Lilac. That would explain the sound of small ghostly footsteps that were known to run up and down the third floor hall.

Lilac couldn't remember the last time she'd set foot on the third floor, now that she thought about it.

"Bram haunts the one spare room on the other side of the landing and Frederick usually stays downstairs."

Lilac had never heard the name Bram before, and she'd never heard Mr. Fright referred to as just "Frederick," either.

"Who are Bram and Frederick?" she asked.

"Oh," Milly clarified. "Mr. Fright's name was Frederick. And Bram is our Butler. But you might not see Bram much, he's a very kind spirit and I don't think he wants to frighten you."

Lilac thought about that for a moment. She'd only seen Bram a few times, and he did seem to disappear just as soon as she saw him. Except for that time with his head on the platter.

"What about you? Where do you like to go?" Lilac asked, although she thought she already knew the answer.

"I like it in here mostly," Milly told her. "It was my bedroom, too, you know," she added quietly after a pause.

Lilac felt a little cold. She hadn't thought about that before, but now she realized that Milly had lived there while she was alive, too. For a while, anyway, until she had died so young, probably no more than eight or nine, Lilac guessed.

"Oh," Lilac said softly, feeling rather terrible about ever having felt possessive of the room or frightened by Milly's presence there. Imagine how that felt to Milly. Still haunting and having another girl move into her space.

"I'm... I'm sorry," Lilac said to Milly. "I didn't know this was your room..."

Milly sat silently, and Lilac said nothing else for a while.

Lilac looked around. It had been her room, but she had spent so little time in it, it all seemed quite unfamiliar, as if it really were more Milly's room than hers anyway. The walls had all been painted the palest purple, and there were carpets over the old scuffed wooden floors that matched. Lilac's mother had picked out the color for her, her father had said. Yet Lilac was never sure if she liked it. It was too pale to be pretty, too dull to be bright and cheerful. It was almost as if it wanted to be a real purple but never would be. Yet it was still purple.

The furniture was at least a hundred years old, like everything else in the house, and based on the layers of paint she could see from a few spots that had chipped off, Lilac knew it had once been white, then light pink, then blue, then yellow, then blue again, and was now a dull, cracked eggshell white. She wondered if it had even been Milly's furniture, and if so, what color it had been. But she didn't ask.

Plop. Tink. A faint sound came from the hallway.

"Come here, Archie," Milly called to her brother. Archie floated through the wall. He had an odd childish grin on his face as he held a large swirled sucker in one hand, and a fistful of jacks and a rubber ball in the other.

"Show Lilac how good you are at jacks," Milly said as she floated off the bed and onto the floor. Archie sat with her, setting his ghostly sucker onto the carpet.

Plop, tink! Archie began to throw his ball and pick up the jacks.

Onesies. Twosies. Threesies. Easy, Lilac thought. Anyone can do that. Then Archie started to pick up speed. Lilac had to admit that he was pretty impressive. He went all the way up to tensies, which is as high as Lilac had ever gone, because like most sets of jacks, Lilac's set only had ten jacks. But Archie's set had thirteen jacks, and he went all the way up to thirteensies. Lilac and Milly clapped and cheered for him when he finished, and Lilac ran into her closet to see if she could find her own set of jacks. She did. Although she couldn't go up to thirteensies like Archie and she was out of practice, Lilac still threw a pretty mean game of jacks. And she'd never played jacks with other children before, and had to admit it was kind of nice. Even though they were ghosts, Lilac realized she was having a lot of fun with Milly and Archie. Like they had become friends.

The three children played for a couple of hours. The time passed slowly as they got to know each other and became more comfortable in the presence of one another. Eventually Archie faded out, using up most of his energy on his haunting game of jacks. Lilac and Milly sat back on the bed together, Milly formed in a barely visible apparition.

Skully Manor was quiet now, with no further outbursts of poltergeist activity. One by one, the news crews and amateur paranormal investigators left.

All of them had driven off. Except one. The white van that had taken the Blue Lady, according to the ghosts, anyway. It was still parked just a ways down the road from Skully Manor, unmarked with no license plate on the front. There were black sunshades drawn over the windshield, and the side windows were tinted dark black. And its presence was unsettling to all of the residents at Skully manor—alive and dead.

Eventually, Lilac began to get sleepy and felt herself doze off. She jolted her head back up and quickly stood up from the bed. Although she was technically in her own bedroom, she'd learned it was also Milly's bedroom, and falling asleep in the same bed as a ghost still felt a little strange.

Lilac walked over to the window and cautiously peered out from the side of the curtain again.

"It doesn't look like anyone's in the van," she observed.

"Oh, they're in there." Milly sighed. "If they aren't, their equipment is," she added, "trying to listen in on all our conversations, you know." She gave a knowing nod to Lilac.

Lilac realized that this must feel weird as a ghost, having paranormal investigators attempting to get a recording of what you're saying or a photograph of you without your permission.

"Hopefully they'll go away soon, now that Mr. Fright has stopped haunting." Milly added.

Lilac hoped so, too.

"Well, I'm getting hungry," Lilac offered as a way to excuse herself. "Maybe I'll go downstairs..."

"Of course," Milly smiled just a little bit and laughed, "Is that why you're always hiding in the kitchen, Lilac

Skully?" she teased. "I've almost forgotten what it's like to eat," Milly lamented.

"Heh!" Lilac tried to laugh back casually, but she felt very awkward. It was often because of Milly herself that Lilac hid out in the kitchen.

"I'm going to get some of my things while I'm up here," Lilac added, trying not to make it sound like she was asking for Milly's permission to get her own belongings out of her own bedroom.

"Oh, of course, that's fine," Milly said politely, and added, "I'm not using any of this stuff."

Lilac went to the closet and pulled out her two warmest sweaters, her sweater dress, her warm pajamas, her wool socks, her hat, her winter jacket, her boots, sweatpants, her gloves, and the extra-warm down quilt from the very top shelf. She wrapped all of the stuff up in the quilt like a satchel and threw it over her shoulder.

"Whelp, I'll see you around!" Lilac said, as friendly as she could to Milly, and headed towards the door.

"See you around, Lilac," Milly replied.

Skully Manor was still and quiet. Lilac tiptoed back downstairs to the kitchen. She locked all of the doors and latches, breathing a heavy sigh before putting her warm things back in the maid's quarters. She set the teakettle on the stove.

It was late afternoon, but after being kept awake all night with Mr. Fright's terrible antics, Lilac found herself exhausted.

Casper was meowing loudly and angrily, as she'd barely given him any breakfast with all the commotion that morning. She apologized and gave him a small plate of canned fish. There was only one tiny portion left. She hadn't eaten all day, either, so she grabbed a handful of crackers and sat down.

"Well," she said out loud, "It was a very strange day," she told her cat in between the crunch of crackers. "I think I made friends with a ghost," she pointed out, crunching some more. "Maybe two." She crunched and nodded her head.

"Well, maybe not, friends, necessarily," she corrected herself. She didn't really know how it would feel to have friends, so she couldn't quite tell.

"But, maybe, they are." She thought about this for a moment. "You know?" she said, somewhat amazed with herself. She had talked with the ghosts. On purpose. And even played with them.

"And the house was on TV," she noted almost unbelievably, "while I watched it live..." Her thoughts drifted as she crunched more crackers.

The kettle boiled, and she poured herself a cup of chamomile. She noticed this was the last clean cup.

The dirty ones had been piling up in the massive, bone-colored porcelain sink, and it had been several days since she'd done any dishes.

"I'll clean up tomorrow," she told herself, as there was no one there to care whether or not Lilac did the dishes.

Lilac took her teacup to her cushioned window seat and curled up with one of her favorite books, *The Little Princess*. She tried to focus on the pages, but her mind wandered back to the white van parked outside, again and again. She wondered if it was still there. And she hoped it would just go away.

9.

The Most Horrible Orb

Bang. Lilac sat up in the pitch dark. She listened. She heard her heart thumping out of control. *Bang.* She tried to hold her breath and not make a sound. She found a moment to wonder how her heart could feel so much like it was in her throat all of a sudden. "Why does it do that?" she thought to herself.

Bang. Bang. She heard again. This banging was not the same rattling bang that Mr. Fright had been making last night. Nor was it like the thunderous banging shutters of the night before that, she thought. This was more like a quiet bang, like a bang that didn't want to be heard.

Lilac sat motionless, ears tuned to any sounds that might come next. She heard a rustling coming from the basement. Then, footsteps. She froze. She wanted to breathe and blink and hide back under the blankets, but she could not move.

The staircase down to the basement was just on the other side of the wall to Lilac's kitchen hideout. So she could hear if anyone—ghost or alive—walked up or down the stairs.

These were the footsteps of a living person. She could tell because of the way the sound echoed off the walls of the house. It wasn't like the hollow, empty, otherworldly sounds of the ghosts. She heard the steps grow louder and ascend the stairs slowly from the basement, one by one.

Creeeeaaaak. She heard faintly. She recognized the sound. It was the door from the first floor of Skully Manor that led to the basement. And it was being opened, ever so gently.

Step, step, step. She heard the footsteps fade out a bit as they walked across the house.

Click! Creeee-craaaaaack. There was a different creak, and she knew it was the front door of Skully Manor.

"Father?" she said in the quietest whisper. "No," she told herself. Her father wouldn't come in from the basement or the front door. He'd drive the car to the back and come in the kitchen like he always did. And he'd say, "Are you still hiding in the closet, Lilac?" as he always did.

Her heart raced and reverberated loudly with each beat. She listened over the sound of her blood rushing like running water through her ears.

"Liii-lac" she heard a quiet voice say. The hairs on her arms began to stand up.

Lilac gulped and closed her eyes. "Milly?" she

whispered back, as quietly as she could.

"There's someone in the house," Milly responded, ever so softly.

Lilac felt like the knot in her stomach was going to suck her into a black hole of everlasting doom. She sat silently, not knowing what to do.

"What should I do?" Lilac finally responded.

"Help us!" Milly said in a strained tone.

Lilac didn't move. She sat and listened for several minutes more.

Silence and then, *Clunk. Clunk. Scrape.* Lilac heard the sound of something rolling through the foyer.

"Liiii-lac!" She heard Milly call her name again, this time more desperate. "It's the men with the Horrible Orb!"

Milly's disembodied voice finally materialized in the dark, just in front of Lilac. She had the faintest blue glow and a panic-stricken look in her dark swirling eyes.

"Do something! Help us!" Milly spoke dramatically. Milly swirled around the room, starting to show her frustration that Lilac wasn't taking any action to help.

"They're trying to capture us," Milly wailed. And again, she disappeared.

Lilac still did not move. She sat in her makeshift bed in the window seat in the back of the kitchen and listened.

When she heard men's voices whispering outside the kitchen doors, she started to sweat and shake.

She almost ran for the back door. Maybe to Mr. Jones's house, or maybe to another neighbor, a mom she'd seen with kids. She wondered if she should have opened the door for the police today and asked for help. She suddenly felt foolish, and very alone.

Rattle, rattle, rattle. The men tried to open the latched swinging doors to the kitchen, pushing on them several times, just a few feet from where Lilac sat.

Tears began to stream down her face, and she could not stop them. Her whole face and neck started to feel wet, but she was too frightened to move or wipe the tears away.

She sat still and listened as the men left the kitchen doors and went back into the house. She heard two men walk down the cellar stairs on the other side of the wall. The sound of them so close caused another rush of fear to well up. She heard loud cracking and banging noises below her. She covered herself in the blankets and made herself as small as possible.

A few moments passed, but it felt like an eternity to Lilac Skully. She heard the footsteps come back up from the basement, the two voices talking in hushed yet excited tones.

Whiiiiir. Lilac heard the sound of machinery being

switched on in the main house.

Clunk, clunk, clunk. Lilac heard the sound going back down the stairs on the other side of the wall. *Swoooosh.* It was not unlike the sound of the vacuum, she thought, but that wasn't quite it.

"Muahahaha!" She heard Mr. Fright call out in an angry maniacal laugh. *Smash. Crash.* There was a commotion below her, almost as if there were a whole bunch of bulls or elephants running around in the basement.

"Liiii-lac!" She heard Milly's voice call out again.

Lilac was still hidden under the blankets.

"Help us!" Milly demanded, this time loudly, then quickly swirled out again.

The whirring noise was continuous and then got louder. One of the men began shouting. Lilac heard a triumphant hoot and holler.

"Liiii-lac!" Milly screamed again. "They've got my brother!"

Lilac looked up and saw Milly hovering over her with a look of pure terror and fright. Lilac scurried backward till she hit the wall behind her. She thought of Archie catching her foot the other night when she almost fell off the roof. He had saved her. She knew she would have been badly injured if she had fallen. And in just the past day of getting to know Milly and Archie, she felt like she might have real friends for the first time in her life. And now, she was letting her friends down.

She jumped out of bed in her pajamas and socks and ran to the kitchen doors. She unlocked the various latches and locks and burst through. Lilac flew through the dining hall with great leaps, her white hair streaking behind her, her feet barely hitting the ground. And she saw the source of the whirring sound in front of her.

It was the Most Horrible Orb, as Milly had called it, and it was indeed, horrible.

The orb was a large glass globe with metal bands arching across it, this way and that. It was sitting on some sort of a makeshift cart with wheels. There was a strange purple glow around it, and it was vibrating, crackling, sparking, and whirring in the middle of the foyer.

And even worse, Lilac saw Archie's face pressed up against the glass inside the orb, calling soundlessly for help. His jacks and rubber ball still clutched in his hands as he banged against the side. Terrible flashes of electricity and light sparked across. Archie's apparition jolted and shook violently with each shock.

There was a long tube that was also lit up with a purple glow and sparking electric bolts. Lilac wondered what it was, and thought it looked very much like a space-age vacuum hose. It was coming out of the base of the orb, and Lilac followed the tube through open doors and down the hallway to the library.

She heard Mr. Fright's voice scream, but not the same loud, cackling, whooping for which he was known. This time, Mr. Fright sounded different, like Mr. Fright was fighting for his life.

Whiir. The whirring noise from the orb picked up in speed and intensity. Lilac gulped. *Crash.* She heard a clatter from the library, followed by the shouts of the two men and the voice of Mr. Fright yelling out again.

Lilac saw the fallen crest of the House of Skully, the one that Mr. Fright had knocked down and tried to smash her with during his poltergeist outburst the other night. Lilac's gaze stopped on the silhouette of two swords crossed behind a terrible human skull on the crest of the House of Skully. The orb sparked and sputtered. Archie jolted inside with each shock of electricity.

Lilac dashed across the room and grabbed one of the swords out of the fallen crest. She really didn't expect it to come loose so easily, but it came out of its sheath with a satisfying "*swoosh*!" and a "*ding!*" as the sharp blade scraped against the metal sheath. The sword was heavy for such a small girl, but Lilac felt a surge of energy and swore she saw silvery sparks as she lifted it up.

With both hands, she held the sword in front of her

and dashed forward. She sliced at the glowing, sparking vacuum tube. She shook as the electricity encircling the tube transferred through her sword and into her body. Her muscles felt like they were stiffening and could not move, much like being held in a ghostly gaze, she thought.

"On the count of three," she said silently, "One, two, three."

Lilac surged and cut the glowing vacuum tube all the way through, severing the grip of electricity and causing the tube to slump to the ground.

She heard frantic shouts come from the library, and then again, the voice of Mr. Fright. But this time it was his usual loud, maniacal, shrieking that she knew all too well.

"Muaaaaaahahahhaha!" Mr. Fright laughed with a ghostly, hollow cackle.

Lilac ran towards the library, brandishing her newfound sword. She pushed through the doors with her shoulder and yelled as loudly as she could. She didn't know what she was doing, and she was very frightened.

"Aaaaaaaaaaaaaah!" Lilac Skully screamed. She looked around the room mid-step and saw two men in black clothes, their faces covered with strange thick goggles and black face masks.

"Get out of my house!" Lilac roared, in a volume

and tone that no one would have expected out of Lilac Skully, not even Lilac herself.

The men exchanged glances, and one of them lunged at Lilac's legs and knocked her down. The other came over and tried to wrestle her sword away, but she held tightly on to its grip. It was a very long sword, and without hesitation, Lilac raised it as high as she could and sliced into the man's leg.

The man screamed and fell to the ground. Blood began pouring out of a gash on his ankle and over his hands as he clutched his leg and moaned.

Mr. Fright's disembodied voice screamed with delight and cheered. The man who had grabbed Lilac's legs was distracted in the panic of the moment. Lilac scrambled upright and braced herself, sword outstretched. She shook, and the sword trembled with her, but Lilac stood her ground.

The injured intruder pulled the mask off his face and held it over the gash, trying to stop the blood. Lilac stared at him.

"Dear.... God!" he cried, exasperated. "Where did this little girl come from?" he winced.

"Let's get out of here!" the other man said and ran from the library out into the hall.

The injured man gasped in pain and yelled again as he stood up and hobbled out of the library. A trail of blood dripped behind him down the hall.

Lilac did not move. She held out her shaking sword, willing to strike at anyone that tried to hurt her.

"Archie!" she heard Milly wailing from the foyer. "Archie!" Milly screamed.

Lilac heard the orb rolling out of the front doors of Skully Manor.

Creeeaaak. Slam. They shut the front door.

Lilac's body fell to the floor in a heap.

Clank. The massive sword fell with her.

10.

The Aftermath

Lilac lay on the floor of the library, staring out into nothingness. Her sword was still held loosely in her hand, the blood from the intruder she sliced was dripping down her arm.

Normally the floor of the library was not a place she would sit and feel sorry for herself because Mr. Fright often haunted there. But right now, Lilac didn't care.

"Liii-lac?" She heard a voice say very gently to her.

"I'm sorry, Milly," Lilac said. "I was too late to help your brother." Tears took over her voice, and her vocal chords shook as she tried to get out the words that she felt. "It's all my fault," she managed to say through a contorted face and a flood of wet tears.

"It's not your fault," Milly tried to reassure her. "They've been coming after us for a while," Milly added. "And it was Mr. Fright who brought all the attention here with his outburst, anyway," she said, shaking her head disapprovingly. "If it's anyone's fault, it's his."

"Oh, don't blame me for this, little girl!" Mr. Fright's crackly, grumbly reply came out from somewhere in the library stacks.

His disembodied voice shocked Lilac back into the moment, and she sat upright, alert.

"We've all been in danger for some time now," Mr. Fright continued, "all of us haunting here," he emphasized and paused, "And I suppose even the little Skully girl's in danger now!" He laughed and cackled one of his frightening maniacal laughs that made Lilac's arm hair stand on end.

"Wh... whaddya mean?" Lilac couldn't believe she was engaging Mr. Fright in conversation, but at this point, she had nothing to lose.

"That was a pretty good *WHACK!* there with that sword, little girl," he said with another laugh. "*SWACK!*" he mimicked and made a loud bang come out of nowhere, one of his poltergeist specialties. "Aaah!" he shrieked and laughed, mocking the man who Lilac had cut with the sword.

"That was a lot of blood!" he then remarked with glee as he recalled the entire gruesome event, finally appearing from the shadows of the room. He swooped in close to Lilac Skully's face.

"You mighta killed him!" he shouted, his musty, cold breath blowing over Lilac, who was already on the ground but scrambled backward with the sound of each word he spoke. Mr. Fright laughed again and swirled up and out of the library. Milly remained silent.

Lilac sat for a few moments with her head in her hands and then stood up. She picked up her sword, and started towards the door.

“Liiii-lac?” Milly asked.

Lilac stopped and turned. “Yeah?” she replied.

“That was a pretty good *whack* with your sword,” Milly said.

Lilac didn’t know what to say.

“I didn’t think you had it in you,” Milly continued, adding a rare smile and a small laugh, “Seeing as you’re just a little girl and all...”

“Thanks,” Lilac sighed, the sword in her hand, the bloody tip resting on the ground. “Um, I’ll see you tomorrow, Milly, okay? And we’ll find a way to get your brother back. I think I’m gonna go back to bed now.” She yawned and motioned towards the clock. “It’s three a.m.”

“See you tomorrow Lilac,” Milly responded, and disappeared.

Lilac retreated to the maid’s quarters in the back of the kitchen and made sure all of the locks on her door were secure.

Her hands shook as she washed the blood off of the sword and off of her hands and arms.

Mr. Fright was right. That was a lot of blood. She imagined herself in jail for the rest of her life. Lilac Skully, Notorious Murderer. She wrapped the sword in an old burlap sack and brought it to the pantry. She lifted the loose floorboard where she'd hidden things for years and slid the sword under the house. She noticed three overdue library books next to the firecrackers she'd also forgotten about.

"Oh dear god," she gasped under her breath. She'd had those overdue books for years. This would drastically affect her chances of becoming a librarian in the future. This was not good. She felt cold and too frightened to cry, even though she wanted to.

She crawled back into her bed and tried to sleep, but the past few days of events and Mr. Fright's words echoed through her ears.

"You mighta killed him!" *Slice...* the sound of her sword. The blood. The overdue library books. Her shattered dreams of becoming a librarian. Lilac replayed these moments over and over in her mind. Mr. Fright's booming voice. Archie's face screaming and shocking inside the orb.

"What have I done?" she whispered into the darkness.

11.

Black, Black, and Gremory

It was nearly ten in the morning by the time Casper woke her up for breakfast. Lilac was ridiculously groggy. She put on the teakettle and emptied out the last bit of fish onto Casper's plate. Her stomach knotted and turned with pangs of acidic hunger. She swallowed hard and filled up a glass with water from the sink, and drank it all.

"Well, I guess I'll be going down into the basement this morning to get our food," Lilac said to Casper.

Going down into the basement didn't sound nearly as scary as usual, not after the past few days of strange and horrifying events, she thought. She'd even talked to Mr. Fright yesterday. And, he didn't kill her.

The kettle whistled, and she poured her cup of tea. She sipped it as she put on her warmest socks, sneakers with laces double knotted, and her coziest wool sweater. She unlatched the kitchen doors that led to the dining room and she stepped into the dining hall.

She walked carefully through the dim and dusty manor so as to not spill her tea, stopping to sip a few times.The morning light was streaming through the cracks on the edges of the dark velvet curtains in the foyer, illuminating drops of blood on the tile and carpets. The bright red blood from last night had started to dry to a more rusty color. Powder from the fire extinguisher still clung to the chandelier and walls. The burnt tablecloths and remains from Lilac's chaotic séance were still scattered around. There were two dirty track marks where the wheels of the ghost-snatching orb had rolled in. The hose that had sucked up Archie still lay on the floor of the foyer and down the hall to the library.

Lilac stood in front of the stairs to the cellar. She sighed and sipped her tea again. The door had been left ajar by the intruders last night. She flicked on the light switch. She took a deep breath and walked down the stairs as quietly as she could.

Going down these very stairs into the basement brought back some of Lilac's most chilling childhood memories. Mr. Fright enjoyed chasing her up the stairs, then slamming the door shut and locking it when she got to the top, so she was trapped. Once, she got stuck downstairs for almost two hours until her father came home and unlocked the door. Needless to say, the cellar was a place she avoided. But this time, it didn't seem quite as bad.

When you got to the bottom of the stairs and stepped into the twisty, twirly, haunted basement of Skully Manor, there was a dark section you had to get through before you could turn on the next light by pulling a string. Lilac went as quickly as she could through the darkness to the next light, and her heart began to thump.

Thump, thump, thump. Lilac felt the same old panic start to grip her. She hurried to the light and pulled the string. The light came on, dimly, yet her fear subsided a bit as she looked around, crouched with her back to the wall.

"Oh no," she whispered as she surveyed the damage that the intruders had caused.

The cellar door in the back corner hung crooked off one of its hinges where they had broken in. The door to her father's research laboratory had also been ripped off. There were papers and shattered glass and electrical equipment strewn everywhere, coming out from the laboratory door and spreading all over the basement in a jumbled mess.

Lilac carefully stepped over the broken objects and walked towards the door of her father's laboratory. She flicked on the lights and peeked in. She sipped her tea.

Lilac had not been in her father's laboratory for many years. Although he spent the majority of his waking hours there, she wasn't allowed. It was for her safety, he'd say, and he kept it under lock and key.

The intruders had ransacked the entire lab. Several pieces of equipment looked like they had been torn right out of the wall, with their electrical wires still exposed. Her father's large file cabinets had been tipped over and dumped. Thousands of pages of his handwritten notes were strewn around the room, inches thick.

Lilac popped her head back out of the lab. She wasn't sure what to do. But she was hungry. She went to the shelves in the cellar where her father kept their supply of food. She set down her teacup and opened the case of orange soda. She popped the top off of a bottle and gulped almost half of it within a few seconds. She saw a box of packaged cookies on the back of the shelf and dove for it, ripped open the box and grabbed a cookie, then shoved it into her mouth with a shaking hand. She sat down and ate a few cookies, washing them down with orange soda.

She took a deep breath and smiled. She suddenly wondered where the ghosts were and what they were doing right now, and why they hadn't come to haunt her yet. But she didn't call out for them. She figured she should try to clean up some of the mess. Some of it was her fault, and even if it wasn't, she had been left responsible for the house.

After eating her fill of cookies, she finished her soda and went back to the laboratory. She knelt down and looked at some of the papers. There were so many. She didn't know where to start. She picked up papers one by one, trying to stack them together if they seemed like they might match.

"Father's notes with dates..." she muttered. "Those are easy." She gathered as many of those together as she could.

"Electricity bills..." A number caught her eye. "Wow, that's a lot," she said. She looked around at the massive stacks of strange looking electrical and scientific equipment her father had in his laboratory. She also thought about all of the times she tried to turn off the lone bulb in the kitchen to save energy.

She picked up another piece of paper.

"Moore, Witts, and Constantine Partners in Law," she read.

"Dear Dr. Skully," it said, "You are hereby served with a lawsuit by our clients represented at Black, Black, and Gremory Paranormal Research Partners..." she continued. "For the patent infringement on US patent #3469999997321," Lilac stopped reading and scanned the page.

"Huh. That's a pretty recent date," Lilac shrugged. "My father never mentioned getting sued..." She set that one down in a pile she'd started for various letters that seemed important. She gathered up another stack and began to go through them.

"Bank statements," she read. "Wow." She looked at the figures on the paper. "That sounds like a lot of money," she said out loud to no one in particular. "Yet here I am, hungry and alone."

"You're not alone," Milly popped out, suddenly. Lilac jumped a bit.

"Oh! Th... thanks for that, I guess," Lilac said, trying not to look like she had been startled. She shuffled the papers in her hand and smiled nervously. "Morning, Milly."

"Morning, Lilac," Milly replied and hung in the air, her feet not quite on the ground. She floated and watched Lilac intently, but didn't say anything. It was a little creepy, but Lilac didn't mention it and continued with what she was doing.

She pulled out another letter that caught her eye. It had been typed up on thicker, cream-colored paper and then folded in thirds to fit in an envelope. There was a raised stamp imprinted by a signature. Lilac's fingers ran over the raised letters.

"Black, Black, and Gremory," she read.

Milly gasped when she heard the name and held her hands to her cheeks. "Oh! Those are the men in the white van!" she said in horror. "Notorious ghost hunters!" she put her hands over her heart and shook her head gently, a faint ghostly dust shimmering around her.

"Dear Dr. Skully," Lilac read the letter. "I'm writing again as I did not receive a response about our generous offer to employ you with a senior position at our research facility. We are willing to negotiate, and we have something of interest here at the laboratory that may persuade you. If you are unwilling to cooperate, we will be forced to take drastic measures, which, may not be in the best interest of you and your family—living and dead. Please come to the laboratories as soon as possible to discuss. Ask for Mr. Gremory at the gate. Regards, Forsyth Gremory." She looked at the very elaborate and inky black signature of Forsyth Gremory.

"Oh," Milly shook her head and tutted. "I'm afraid this means your father is a very bad man."

"It doesn't mean... that," Lilac stammered. "I've heard that name, and I know..." Admittedly, Lilac didn't know much at all about what her father did.

"I'm pretty sure he wasn't friendly with them." Lilac continued and motioned to the paper. "It even says here, my father didn't want the job." She nodded, feeling satisfied in her defense. "And it sounds like they might have been threatening him," she said, although she didn't really understand what the letter meant.

"And," Lilac added, "I heard him talk on the phone once about Mr. Gremory," she said in a serious tone. "And it wasn't good." Lilac didn't want to continue.

"Well, what did he say?" Milly asked.

"That they weren't..." Lilac shook her head and stopped.

"Weren't what!" Milly demanded.

"Weren't respectful of the dead." Lilac said darkly. Milly did not respond.

Lilac picked up another letter that was on the same stationery and had the same seal of Black, Black, and Gremory.

"Dear Dr. Skully," Lilac read again. "Due to the highly illegal nature of your recent work, you leave us no choice but to contact the authorities. If you would like to discuss..." Lilac stopped reading.

"What does that mean?" Milly asked.

"I'm not sure," Lilac replied, putting that letter into her folder. "But I think my dad was in big trouble." She sorted through a few more papers, unable to concentrate on what they said. She was still trying to process all of the information she had just read. It was too much. She put the folder of papers she'd collected into a filing cabinet and shut the drawer.

"And maybe that's why I have to take care of everything here." Lilac said with a sigh.

She was just about to go upstairs, realizing there wasn't anything she could do to fix what had been destroyed in his laboratory. She felt more frustrated and confused than ever.

Bleep! Blee-boop, blee-boop! Squeeeee! A cracked monitor on the floor lit up and came to life, squeaking and beeping. Lilac sprang backward, wishing she had brought the sword downstairs with her.

"Hello? Hello?" a familiar voice called out through the static.

Lilac stepped over a pile of papers and approached the monitor and the equipment attached to it.

"Hello?" it said again.

The shape of a blurry green head blinked in and out, struggling to appear on the monitor.

"Lilac?" the voice said and the screen blinked a few more times. Eventually, a face fuzzed into focus on the green-tinged monitor.

It was her father.

12.

Ghosts in the Cellar

"F*ather?*" Lilac cried out in disbelief.

"Lilac!" her father's eyes smiled at the sight of her coming through on his monitor.

"Where *are* you!" she gasped, her hands at her hips, her brow furrowed in deep disappointment.

"I don't have time to explain," he said through the cackling static.

"We've been *starving*!" She threw one hand up and shook her head, eventually crossing her arms as her father tried to explain.

"Lilac, now listen to me, and I'll be able to get out of here quickly." He brought his face closer to the monitor.

Lilac looked at him carefully. She wasn't sure if his glasses were cracked and if he had a bruise under his eye, or if it was just the static coming over the thick green monitor glass. Lilac listened. He paused and looked past her quizzically. He pulled closer to the screen.

"Is that..." he said, sidetracked. "Fascinating!" he cried. "Lilac, the Little Girl Ghost is standing right behind you!"

"I know!" Lilac replied, annoyed.

Her father hastened his pace and got back on track. He seemed a bit flustered.

"Lilac," he said seriously. "The Manor was broken into last night, and half of this communication system was taken."

"I know!" Lilac replied again, exasperated. She knew quite well. She had been there—alone and terrified—the entire time.

"And my brother was kidnapped!" Milly cried out.

Dr. Skully's eyes lit up as if he hadn't heard the terrible thing she had said at all.

"Ah, it seems the ghost communication system is in full working order!" He seemed very pleased. He straightened his glasses and fussed with his hair.

"And lucky for us," he replied, "because I'm able to deliver this very important message to you" He pushed his glasses up on his nose. Lilac did not respond.

"They'll be coming back tonight for the other half of this communicator," her father said through the monitor, a little bit quieter as he quickly looked over his shoulder to the side. "And I need you to make absolutely certain to..."

BLEEP! Blink, blink, squee, zonk. The monitor flicked off.

Lilac gasped and knelt down. She shook the monitor

with both hands.

"What!" she cried. "What do I need to make absolutely certain to do?" She wiggled the cords and shook the monitor again.

"Father!" she called into it once more. The screen stayed black.

She sat back for a moment and shook her head. "What could he want?" she said. "Father must want me to hide the rest of the equipment and make sure they don't get it." Lilac guessed. "What else could it be?" she sighed and grabbed her head with both hands. "I wish he hadn't left me here, responsible for everything!" she sat back. "I'm just... a little girl." she said.

Milly gave her a long stare. "At least you're not going to get sucked up in that horrible orb tonight," she wailed, "like meeee."

"Well!" Mr. Fright's voice and a swift chill came out of nowhere. "Are the little girls having a bad day already?" Mr. Fright swooped in through the wall and cackled. "Let's see if I can make it even worse!" he clapped.

"Oh leave us alone!" Milly said back. "Lilac got you out of the orb last night."

It was true. He owed her one. But there was no way Lilac was going to tell him that to his face.

"Sounds like the famous Dr. Skully is involved with the ghost-nappers!" Mr. Fright laughed and cackled.

"No!" Lilac replied instantly. "Why would my father break into his own house? That doesn't make any sense."

"All I know is they've got my brother!" Milly wailed. "And now they're coming back..." She paused, and her voice trembled off. "For meeee!" She gasped deeply and brought her hands back up to her cheeks in horror, then floated backward.

"But... where is my father?" Lilac stammered. "And why did he leave me? Why hasn't he come home yet?" Lilac's tone shifted. She crossed her arms again and looked down at everything strewn about his strange, ransacked laboratory.

"Why can't he just have a regular, boring job like everyone else!" she said.

Milly was not listening. She was panicking and wailing and carrying on about being captured.

"Better get your bloody sword out and get ready to fight, Little Girl Skully!" Mr. Fright cackled again. "They're coming back!" His signature spooky laugh echoed through the basement, "Bwahaha ha ha!"

"Well, they're coming for you, too!" Lilac called back to him. "So you'd better help!" She nodded adamantly.

"Help what?" Mr. Fright's gruesome, sour face appeared right in front of Lilac.

"Help us defend Skully Manor!" Lilac said without flinching.

Mr. Fright's face sank. "Aren't you going to run and hide from me, anymore, Little Girl Skully?" He laughed and cackled inches from her face. She could smell his pale earthy breath.

"No." She said and folded her arms. She knew her lower lip and voice were trembling, but she continued. "Are you going to help or not?" she asked, looking him straight in the eyes.

"You'll never catch me walking right into that confounded ghost trap again," he said, indignantly. "How stupid do you little girls think I am?" And he swirled away, whipping up the papers Lilac had organized, and scattering them all around the room again.

"I'm doomed!" Milly cried and wailed louder, floating up and around the lab in dramatic cold swooshes of air, and then sank into a corner and cried.

"I'll help you, Milly." Lilac said to try to calm her down.

"And I'll help you, too," a different soft voice called out of nowhere, startling Lilac again. An apparition gently appeared before her. Lilac was taken aback.

"I won't harm you, Miss Skully," the ghost said and gave a slight bow to Lilac.

"The Butler," Lilac said under her breath.

“My name is Bram,” he replied. “And I apologize for the time I scared you with my head on the platter,” he tried to explain while stifling a smile. “It was your dastardly tutor I was trying to scare off, and not you, Miss.”

The corners of Lilac’s mouth turned up a bit, and she giggled.

“I’ve only seen you a few times,” Lilac said in disbelief, although he was clearly standing before her now, in a crisp bluish apparition, having an intelligent conversation with her.

“The Butler,” as he was known, was a famous ghost of Skully Manor that Lilac had only seen a few times in her nine and three-quarters years. Like his nickname suggested, he looked just as you might expect a Victorian Butler to look. Tall, slim, short dark hair that had been slicked back neatly, and a puffy, elaborate mustache that had been precisely shaped. He wore a dapper uniform with a vest and a long-tailed coat. He had a pocket watch and chain, and a pair of immaculate white gloves.

“I’ve stayed out of your sight as much as possible. I did not wish to frighten you, Miss Skully,” he said and smiled. “Unlike some ghosts,” he said as he looked up and around, “who get a real big kick out of haunting little girls.” He rolled his eyes.

Mr. Fright's dreadful laugh boomed through the basement, and although it made Lilac jump, the other ghosts laughed, and Lilac found herself laughing, too.

"I think I'm going to go upstairs and have some breakfast," Lilac announced, suddenly feeling very hungry. "Then let's meet again and plan for tonight."

"Tonight?" Milly asked.

"My father said they were coming back, didn't he?" Lilac replied.

Milly nodded, a terrified look in her swirling dark eyes.

"Then we're going to be ready," said Lilac Skully.

13.

The Best Laid Plans of Ghosts and Little Girls

She made several trips up and down the basement stairs, carrying up some cans of fish for Casper, several boxes of crackers, her orange soda, a few cans of chili and string beans, and a gigantic jar of generic peanut butter and one of grape jam.

As usual, Mr. Fright tried to slam the door and lock her in, but this time, Lilac Skully was ready. She'd stuck a piece of clear cello tape of the lock of the door handle at the top of the stairs, foiling his haunt.

"Ha!" was all she said to him as she opened the door and stepped through.

Back in her kitchen, she realized she was hungrier than she thought. She scarfed down ten or fifteen crackers with peanut butter and jam, and then opened up another bottle of orange soda, which wasn't even cold yet, and took a sip. She gave Casper a large plate of food, for which he was very grateful.

She sipped her orange soda, as her mind raced. It was the first time she'd had a moment to process what had been going on. And it was a lot. What was her father doing? Why did he leave her all alone? Was he in trouble? Would he go to jail? What would happen to her if he did? She shook her head. This was no way for a father to behave. She thought about how much she'd been through in the past couple days. And now, the burglars were coming back. And she was expected to deal with it. On her own.

The break-in the night before had been terrifying. She remembered how helpless she felt the moment she first heard the men in her house, how she just wanted to run and hide somewhere safe, but there was nowhere else for her to go.

She heard a quiet voice on the other side of the door from the dining room.

"Liiii-lac?"

"Come in, Milly," Lilac responded.

Milly appeared through the door.

"Your correspondence course paperwork has been sitting in the mailbox for three days," she said to Lilac.

"Oh, thank you!" Lilac responded politely. "I'll have to go get that and fill it out..." She added. Lilac liked to finish her home school correspondence coursework as quickly as possible and all in one day, so she'd have the rest of the week to do just as she pleased. It wasn't always that way. She used to work on it meticulously and for hours every day. But then she realized that she got the same marks whether or not she put in the extra effort, so she eventually stopped trying as hard. However, this week, Lilac had completely forgotten.

"I've been busy this week." she said as an excuse for herself and hopped off of her kitchen stool. She took out a notebook and pencil from the pantry. She brought it back to the counter and sat back down.

"Bram said he'd help us," Lilac reminded Milly.

"I can go find him," Milly started to fade out.

"Um..." Lilac hesitated, "Let's meet out at the dining table," she offered, not wanting the ghosts to get too comfortable in her kitchen. Milly nodded and sank backward. Lilac hopped off of her stool and unlatched the latches on the door to the dining room. She made sure to close the open blind so no one could see in and spy on her important meeting with the ghosts. She sat down at the head of the very long table.

Milly and Bram appeared in the doorway of the room.

"May we join you, Miss Skully?" Bram asked.

"Of course!" Lilac waved her hand out for them to join her and they floated closer. She wondered if they thought it was rude because she hadn't set out the candles and the inviting atmosphere for them like in the séance. She hoped not.

"Well?" Lilac tapped her pencil against the blank paper. "First, my father's gear. He said they're coming for the other half of that communicator, so I'm going to make sure that they won't find it." She nodded her head since that made a lot of sense and wrote that down on the piece of paper. "That's the easy part."

"And they'll probably be coming after you guys," she said to the ghosts, "assuming they've attached another hose to the orb," she said, remembering the hose that was still downstairs from when she'd sliced through it with the sword. "We need to be ready for that, anyway." She tapped her pencil and paused.

"Hmm..." Lilac didn't know where else to start or what to do. She got a sinking feeling that planning the counterattack was going to be harder than she thought. How was she supposed to anticipate what the intruders were going to do? And, she was dealing with professional ghost hunters. They weren't going to be afraid of the same "typical" haunting, wailing, spooking, and simple appearing that would scare off most people from Skully Manor.

"I guess they'll come through the basement again," she figured. "since last time they broke into the basement, and the door is still broken," she recalled.

"Well," Lilac thought for a moment, "I wonder if they'll chase me? Maybe I can lead them in the opposite direction from you guys, and then one of you can close the door and trap them in."

Milly and Bram looked at each other.

"I'm afraid neither of us are poltergeists," Bram said as he shook his head. "And I don't think we're going to get Mr. Fright's cooperation on this," he sighed. "I've already been down to try and reason with him..." Bram's face turned to one of exasperation. "He simply refuses to work together on anything. Even if it's in his own self interest." He shook his head.

"He'd just have to shut a door!" Lilac stammered. "I thought he liked slamming doors?!"

"I agree, Miss Skully," Bram nodded, "he does. But we are talking about Frederick Wright, and as you may have noticed, he's not a reasonable ghost."

Lilac wobbled her head back and forth a bit and set her elbows on the table, then held her head in her hands.

"I could tie a string to the doorknob and pull it shut myself," Lilac suggested.

"But then you'd be trapped in there with them!" Milly exclaimed.

"What do you plan to do once you've led them through the manor and have them trapped?" Bram interjected.

Lilac stopped. That was a good point. She wasn't planning to kill them with her sword, nor did she want to trap them and then get the police involved. The last thing she wanted was to rat herself out as an unsupervised child.

"Since they're after you guys," she said, "can't you just disappear from wherever they are and hide?"

"They can see us with those silly bug-eyed goggles," Milly explained. "And we can't wander from the manor," she said nervously.

"The suction on that dreadful contraption is too powerful," Bram shook his head. "I barely got out of it in time." He clasped his hands behind his back. "They sucked up Frederick from three rooms away," he added and motioned across the dining room and towards the main house with one hand. "Unfortunately it seems as if they know our limitations." He sighed.

"They couldn't reach me in the attic." said Milly, remembering her experience the night before. She had been just out of reach up there. "But they found Archie hidden in the cellar." She started to tremble at the thought of her brother getting sucked up by that awful contraption.

"Hmm," Lilac said. "I guess we'll just have to make it as difficult for them as possible. And hide the things they want to take." She nodded. "You guys and my father's equipment." She drew a couple of pictures of ghosts on the paper.

Lilac tapped her pencil again. "Maybe if I can disable the orb right away." That sounded like the most realistic plan so far. "There were a lot of wires and things around the orb," Lilac remembered. "I'll get some wire cutters, and maybe I can break it before they're able to suck you guys up." She thought and wrote "wire cutters" on the paper. "Maybe I can smash the glass orb with a hammer and shatter it..." She wrote "hammer" on the piece of paper. "What did you do with the police radio, Milly? And the lights?" Lilac asked.

"Oh, I can do a few things with electronics and frequencies," Milly nodded, almost forgetting the importance of these abilities.

"What about the orb? It's electric or something. Do you think you can interfere with it from a distance?" Lilac asked.

"That orb was something else," Bram shook his head. "Designed to withstand interference from ghosts, from what I can tell."

"Can you work a walkie-talkie?" Lilac asked.

"Most ghosts can do that," Bram replied.

"I'll put a walkie-talkie in the attic for you guys and take one with me," Lilac told them and wrote "walkie-talkies" on her paper.

"You guys can keep watch upstairs, out of reach from the orb. And when you see the van pull up, give me the signal." Lilac said to them, a bit of a plan starting to formulate as she wrote some notes and drew pictures of walkie-talkies.

"What else can you guys do?" Lilac asked, looking for anything that could help them. Bram looked uncomfortable and didn't say anything.

"Tell her, Bram," Milly said to him.

"I've got a few talents in..."

"Serving your head on a platter?" Lilac interjected dryly, remembering her most frightening encounter with Bram.

"Yes, well, talents in apparitions, but I'm afraid those won't frighten these particular ghost hunters. They're experts." He stopped. "But," he continued. "I'm also able to perform a type of possession, Miss Skully," Bram muttered.

"Possession?" Lilac asked, shocked. "Like... possessing people and making them move and do things against their will?" She stared at him, wide-eyed.

"Yes, or animals." Bram added shyly. "It's an art form that's often misunderstood. And it takes an immense amount of energy. But, it can be done."

"Wow," Lilac said and thought, tapping her pencil against her lower lip. "Well, I guess there's probably something we can do with that..."

By the time they had come up with the ideas for

traps that would keep the burglars away from the ghost hideout in the attic, it was late afternoon. Lilac got to work setting the trip lines and wires that Milly was going to electrify. They tested out the radio system and the cues for Milly to turn different lights and speakers on and off in the house.

Lilac rummaged through the kitchen drawers and took out the walkie-talkies, some batteries, matches, a flashlight, and any tools that looked dangerous, sharp, or useful. She liked her idea of using a rope to pull things, so she found a good length of rope and set up a couple of contraptions around the manor, including an ancient suit of armor that slashed with a butcher's knife, and a cement yard figurine that swung through the foyer from the second floor.

Lilac went back to her father's lab and carefully unplugged the communicator and monitor. Her father said the thieves were after the equipment, so she would hide them in the kitchen to thwart their plans. Bram went down to the cellar to plead with Mr. Fright again for his help, but Mr. Fright refused. Dark clouds rolled in for another round of storms. Night fell early. Bram and Milly set up watch in the attic, as far as they could be from the suction hose of the orb.

Lilac packed up her backpack with walkie-talkies, various tools, matches, and other items she thought she might need. She lifted the loose floorboard in the pantry and carefully took out the sword. She reached in further and pulled out the firecrackers and added those to her bag. She lowered the pieces of her father's lab equipment down under the floorboards, where they "plunked" quietly onto dirt. She replaced the floorboard.

Skully Manor fell still and silent. Lilac walked calmly out of the kitchen and up the stairs to the large second-floor landing that overlooked the foyer of Skully Manor.

She hid behind the tufted sofa, her sword at the ready.

"Lights off!" she said into her walkie-talkie.

All of the bulbs in Skully Manor went off at once. Lilac felt a deep chill as she waited in the darkness.

14.
The Chase

To her dismay, Lilac fell asleep. She was jolted awake by the sound of the walkie-talkie and Bram's calm voice coming through the static.

Bee-boop!

"The van just pulled up, Miss Skully," *Beep. Beep.*

Lilac replied through her walkie-talkie, "Okay." Lilac waited.

Beep. "The men are approaching..." Bram's voice said. "No sign of the orb yet," he added, "but they're rolling something smaller, perhaps just a valise."

Lilac wasn't sure what a valise was, but this did not seem the time to ask.

"This might be easier than we thought," she said to herself in a quiet, confident whisper.

"They're walking around to the back." Bram said, "And ... cue the lights, Milly!"

All of the lights in Skully Manor turned back on. Lilac didn't hear anything out of the ordinary yet. She waited. She closed her eyes to listen harder. The sound of muffled men's voices could just barely be heard the cellar. She guessed they were in the lab and were wondering where the equipment had gone.

"Ha," she said to herself, very pleased. "I hid it, and they'll never find it." She smiled in the dark.

She spoke into her walkie-talkie, *Beep!* "Bram, cue the bats and rats!"

The "bats and rats" was one of the defensive tactics that Lilac and the ghosts had planned. The idea was that Bram would possess the packs of bats or rats living in the walls of the manor and have them swoop in and attack the intruders. Lilac loved this idea.

All of a sudden she heard a tremendous clatter from the basement. There were shrieks and yells and banging. Lilac couldn't help but giggle. She imagined the men being chased by a pack of violent, snarling rats as she listened to them *thump, thump, thump*, and scream in distress, trying to figure out what was happening.

"Geeze Louise! They're vicious! They're climbing up my clothes! Get 'em off me!" She heard strained voices calling from the cellar.

Lilac scrunched her face as she heard the commotion continue.

"Get upstairs!" A man shouted.

"I can't get them off me!" She heard them yell and fall over each other in the scurry of wailing and possessed rats, and then their footsteps finally started to ascend the stairs.

"Gaah, it bit my face!" She heard one of them yell out in a painful cry.

Lilac listened intently. The freakish sound of clawing, snapping rats grew closer as they stomped up, stair by stair.

"Waaaah!" one yelled in a panic.

"Oh crimeny son of a biscuit... something just hit me! Was that a flying rat?" said a breathy, freaked-out voice.

"That was a bat, you idiot!" the other yelled back.

An unearthly chattering and chirping sound could be heard. "Yep, it's the bats," Lilac whispered.

"It bit me! It bit me! I'm gonna die of rabies! Oh, god, help me!" She heard one of the men scream.

The sounds of the two men struggling up the stairs amidst a scurry of possessed, swooping bats and rats was now so gruesome that Lilac closed her eyes and tried to ignore it.

Beep! She spoke into her walkie-talkie again, "Milly, cue the electricity!" she said.

"Open the door, dangit! Open the door!" she heard as the men reached the top landing of the cellar stairs.

Milly had electrified the door handle, and Lilac waited excitedly for the moment that one of them tried to open it, to see if that part of the plan would work.

Zip Zap. Spat.

"Aaaaaaahrrrrrgh!" one of the men yelled in pain, now directly below her at the door that came up from the basement. Lilac's eyes widened as she listened to the long, painful scream of the man.

The zapping and screaming and the sound of the rats and raging bats went on, as long as Milly and Bram had the energy, Lilac supposed. It was a terrible sound, she thought to herself, especially with the squeaking of the rats still audible over the zip and zap of the electricity.

Lilac snapped to attention. The animals and the zapping stopped. The men opened the door and scuffled through, the slammed it behind them in a panicked frenzy. They were just below her in the foyer. She held her breath.

"Who's in here?" Lilac heard a man's panting, angry voice say, but she could not yet see him. "Little girl?" he called out.

Lilac did not move or twitch. She had positioned herself so she could see under the sofa and between the banister rails at a good portion of the foyer. The men stepped farther into the room, and Lilac could see they were wearing the same ghost-vision goggles like they had last time. She couldn't quite tell if they were the same two men, or if she had killed one of them with her sword. They hadn't screamed like that man had screamed. She gulped. That means she had probably killed him, she reasoned.

The men slowly circled through the foyer, listening to see if anyone was there. They didn't have a giant orb like last time, but both of the men were rolling boxes on wheels behind them. Whatever they were, they were too low to the ground, and Lilac couldn't get a good look.

Suddenly, Lilac saw one of the men's legs swing up violently and kick the other square in the rear.

"Crimeny! What the devil!" the man who was kicked said.

"I, I dunno, boss, my leg just spasmed!" the other man said.

Lilac's eyes widened. She wondered if it was Bram, possessing them.

Schwap. The man who had been kicked spun around, his arm outstretched at an unnatural angle, and slapped the other in the face.

Lilac broke out into a bit of a smile. It had to be Bram.

Shocked at what had just happened, the man touched his face and stammered.

"You slapped me?" he said.

"My arm just took off on its own!" the man who had slapped him said.

"Oh come on!" the other rolled his eyes incredulously. "Like that would happen!"

"Oh but your leg just spasmed, huh?" the other said back. "Then why not my arm?"

The two men argued for a moment, and Lilac was not sure if they were going to break out into a full-blown fistfight. And then one of them took a few steps back. Lilac had to cover her mouth and stifle the sound of a gasp.

The thing he was pulling on wheels looked like it had a large glass bubble on top, with a cage made of metal strips crisscrossing over it.

Portable Horrible Orbs. Lilac thought in one of those cold, sinking thoughts that rattle you to the core as soon as you think it. She and the ghosts hadn't thought of this. In fact, their whole plan was constructed on the fact that the ghost-sucking hose of the orb could only reach so far.

"Change of plans," Lilac said to herself under her breath and thought very hard about what she needed to do next. She knew she needed to tell the ghosts right away, but she couldn't get through to them without beeping on the radio or going upstairs to find them. Bram might have already seen them up close if he had peeked in, out of sight of their goggles. She had no choice but to wait and deter the men from going upstairs.

"He said no one would be here," one man said to the other, apparently a bit confused by the lights and defenses they had put in place. "He said just come in and take it," he added, a bit bewildered.

"Let's get what we need and get out of here," the other replied.

"What'll it be first, boss?" the first man asked. "Ghosts or gear?"

"Ghosts." the second said. "Since the gear seems to have disappeared..."

Lilac's guts sunk. Her eyes closed. She felt weak. She took a deep breath. The men started towards the stairs that led to the second floor and the Hall of the Little Girl Ghost.

Three. Two. One. Lilac counted to herself. She raised her sword up and sliced the rope that was holding back the cement angel statue. It was actually an old pet cemetery marker that she took from the yard, which she intended to put back just as soon as she was finished with it.

Swoosh. Thwack.

"Aaaarrgh!"

Lilac hit one of them square in the head with the grave marker.

Flump. He fell to the floor unconscious.

"What the..." the other man yelled as he put his hands up to protect his head and looked up at the banister and second-floor landing.

"Jerry?" He shook the man on the floor, who didn't respond.

"Who's up there!" he yelled. "I know you're there!"

Lilac stayed as still and silent as possible. The grave marker swung on the rope, a slight *creak, creak, creak,* as it went back and forth.

The conscious man left the unconscious one on the floor and started up the staircase. If Lilac didn't move fast, he'd see her hiding.

She did not hesitate. She struck a match and lit the first string of firecrackers. She threw it over the banister with a smooth toss in the direction of the man.

Crack! Crack! Crack!

It caught the man off-guard, and she came out from behind the sofa as stealthily as she could. She slipped into the nearest doorway, the guest bedroom at the top of the landing.

"Little girl!" She heard him call. "I know you're up here!" His voice grew louder.

She slid behind the open door in the bedroom and pressed up against the wall, peering out of a tiny crack. She saw the man pass by the door, and she felt a wave of relief.

But he was headed straight towards the staircase to the third floor, which would bring him to the tower attic where the ghosts were hiding. She began to feel cold. She had to keep him away from the ghosts, and preferably to the trip wire that would send him back downstairs, head over heels. She darted out from the bedroom.

"Hey, Mister! I'm over here!" Lilac yelled. The man did not turn around.

"I'm not falling for that," he called back as he marched down the hall.

Lilac stammered. "I'll cut you!" she yelled at him, holding her sword out. The man did not stop. He headed straight towards the third floor stairs. She panicked. She had to tell the ghosts.

Beep. Lilac yelled into her walkie-talkie. "You guys need to get outta there! Now! He's got a portable orb!"

Beep.

The man finally turned around. "Thanks for reminding me, little girl," he laughed. He reached down and pulled a cord sharply on the wheeled box, and the orb on the back of it lit up with the same dull, sparking purple glow.

Whiiir, the portable orb began.

The man unhooked a suction hose from the side of the machine and held it up in the air, whirring.

"Now, I just need to find the ghosts," he laughed again. "Any clues?"

Before Lilac could respond, his arm jolted forward in

a spasm, and the suction hose of the orb stuck straight to his forehead.

"Blaaaaaaargh!" the man yelled as he tried to pull off the sparking suction hose with both hands.

Lilac lunged towards him and lifted her sword. She smashed it down as hard as she could on his portable orb, hoping to slice the suction tube and damage whatever else she could.

She felt her body seize up with electricity and start to shake in a fitful rhythm as the metal blade hit the orb. She couldn't move her arms, and although she wanted to drop the sword, she could not let go. Her rubber-soled sneakers were not enough to keep her from conducting electricity right through. She tried to loosen all of her muscles and drop it but her hands were stuck. Just as she thought she might burst, her hands released the sword and broke the electrical circuit. The sword clattered to the floor as she fell. The orb sputtered but continued to spark and whir.

Lilac reached for her sword, but it was just out of her grasp. The man swooped his hand down and picked it up.

"Now get outta my way, little girl!" he yelled, jerking his equipment back upright and starting again towards the staircase.

Lilac stood up and wobbled. She reached for a bowl

of decorative papier-mâché fruit. She grabbed several pieces, tucking a few under her arm and darted towards the man. She grabbed the large brass candlestick that was also on the table, in case she needed a weapon.

Clunk. Clunk. He pulled the heavy-wheeled orb up the stairs, one step at a time.

The man's large body and the portable orb filled the width of the creaky wooden staircase.

Clunk. Clunk. He pulled the weighty orb up another two stairs.

Lilac darted forward and reached up. She tossed a papier-mâché orange into the suction hose of the portable orb.

Thwoop.

Weeeeee.

"What the heck is going on with this thing?" the man exclaimed when he realized his ghost-hunting machine was malfunctioning.

Lilac ran back around the corner and into her bedroom.

The man went back downstairs, flung the orb on its side and turned it off. He shook the tube, looked inside it, and tried to dislodge the papier-mâché orange that Lilac had clogged it with.

While he was distracted, Lilac had a chance to get back on the walkie-talkie.

Beep!

"Ghosts, come in," she said in a loud whisper. But there was no response. She spoke through it anyway, hoping they could still hear her.

Beep!

"They've got portable orbs!" Lilac tried to catch her breath enough to get the words out clearly. "I knocked out one of the guys, and I'm trying to break the orbs. I might've got one of them clogged up at least," She waited for a response and didn't get one. "But I don't know how long I can hold them off," she continued and waited for a response through the radio. But she didn't hear one. She heard something else.

"Waaaaaah!" she heard the man yelling from the hall. Then, there was the sound of big, heavy, stomping footsteps. She peeked through the crack of the door and saw the man heading towards the second-floor railing.

"Whooaaa!" He was moaning and walking zombie-like, with his arms outstretched in front of him, his stiff legs slowly stomping forward while he gave out unearthly guttural yells.

Lilac was not sure what was happening until he reached the edge of the top floor banister.

"Nooooo!" the man tried to yell, but his body would not stop moving. Bram had possessed him again, Lilac realized, and was leading him straight over the banister rail.

Thud. The man fell to the hard tile floor of the foyer below. Lilac ran and picked up her sword where the man had dropped it.

Blink. All of the lights in Skully Manor went off at once and fell to pitch black. Lilac went into her backpack and got out the flashlight, but she didn't turn it on yet.

"Jerry!" she heard the man who had fallen over the railing yell to his unconscious friend in a moan. "Jerry, get up! Let's find the gear and get out of here."

Jerry moaned but did not move. The other one stood and headed back down to the basement.

Thunk. Whack. Fwump. Bump. Bump. Bump. Bump.

"Aaaaaaah!" The intruder had hit the trip wire at the top of the stairs. Lilac smiled. She hadn't been sure if that had worked over the sound of the rats as they were coming up.

"Aaaah!" She heard him wail again much softer when he finally got to the bottom.

Lilac slid down the banister. She hopped off and flew across the foyer, slammed the basement door shut and locked him in the cellar.

Beep.

Lilac spoke into the walkie-talkie. "I've got one of them locked in the basement!" she cried excitedly, a huge surge of energy and adrenaline rushing through her. “If you can hear me, cue the bats and rats again!” her voice raised with excitement. “I’m gonna go deal with the unconscious one and try to break his portable orb!” She spun around lightly on one sneaker, sword in hand, feeling weightless and unstoppable.

“You think so, little girl?” the second man said, standing right in front of her, no longer unconscious.

Thwack.

Lilac’s vision went dark. Blackness turned to glowing purple swirls. She heard bloopy voices, as bright white lights began to swirl in with the purple. Lilac lay motionless on the floor of the foyer, knocked out cold.

15.
The Flashback

The white and purple swirling lights in Lilac's head fuzzed into focus. Suddenly, she was in the lunchroom of the public school that she attended for a short while, several years ago in the first grade.

"Hazel!" Lilac heard a boy shout at full volume.

"That's her! The freaky girl from the haunted house!" He lowered his voice to a raspy whisper and leaned into his sister a bit, "Her mom diiiiied in there!" he said, drawing out the word "died" dramatically, and widening his eyes.

Lilac froze. She didn't look up but knew for certain that he was pointing at her. A rigid finger, quivering slightly with the exuberance of discovery, shaking his sister's arm vigorously with his other hand.

Hazel's eyes followed her brother's finger, her mouth mid-bite, agape.

"Look at her weird white hair!" he added with a chuckle.

Lilac could smell the tuna fish sandwiches in the twin's lunchbox as she tried to come up with a plan. She knew she was about to be teased, mercilessly, and had no resources or defenses. Should she pack up her lunchbox and the books she'd taken out to read during lunch and run? Should she try to leave the table unnoticed and stand nonchalantly by a teacher?

"Oh." Hazel chewed her tuna fish sandwich as she assessed Lilac, looking her up and down. "This is bad," Hazel said. Her head shook side to side, and she put the sandwich down.

Lilac tried to stand, and her foot got stuck on the bench. She tried to shove her beloved books into her bag, but the corners were getting stuck on the straps as her arms trembled.

"I've heard about you!" Hazel slammed down the Hawaiian punch that was in her other hand and stood up. "We can't have that haunted house freak sitting at our lunch table!"

"I..." Lilac stammered, "I wasn't even sitting at your table!"

Hazel lunged.

Lilac grabbed her book bag and ran, forfeiting her father's old rusty tin lunchbox and the apple and piece of cheese on white bread that she had at the table.

"Get back here, you freak!" Hazel yelled.

"You left your lunch, freak!" Finn called out as he picked up the large red apple and hurled it across the lunchroom at Lilac as she tried to flee to safety.

Finn wasn't smart, and he wasn't nice. But he had good aim, as he'd been raised playing sports. He flung the apple with enough force and trajectory that it hit Lilac square in the head. And her head hit the corner of the lunchroom door.

Lilac hadn't quite realized yet what had happened. Her body suddenly hit the tile floor of the cafeteria, which felt cold. Something warm was running down her head, almost like a hand touching her. It was blood. Her head had hit the door at such an angle to cause a deep gash, which bled profusely.

She curled into a ball. Things started to happen around her. Hazel and Finn vanished. Girls around her were crying. She felt the presence of several teachers and adults. Her teacher, who was a kind and caring woman, knelt down and tried to talk to Lilac in a soothing voice, but Lilac did not respond.

As they waited for the ambulance, one of the school staff came and asked the teacher about Lilac's father, and how to get a hold of him. They said they'd tried to ring his number, but he did not answer. They were going to send someone to Lilac's house to see if anyone was home.

Lilac almost told them that it was useless. Her father was down in his laboratory and would not be emerging till 7:00 or 8:00 p.m. at the earliest. But she didn't say anything. Her eyes were closed, but the tears still squeezed through, since they had nowhere else to go.

Getting called out for being different at the lunch table was enough to put Lilac into a panic. But then to have an apple thrown at her, causing her to hit her head and acquire a serious gash that needed stitches was all too much.

To make matters worse, her father did not come to pick her up from the hospital until almost ten hours later. She waited there alone after her head was stitched up, the nurses in the hospital beginning to worry if the strange little girl with white hair would ever be picked up at all.

"It's the Skully girl," she heard the nurses whisper to each other, then give quiet, tutting sounds and reassuring nods to each other, as if it was understood that there was something incredibly strange and sad about Lilac, just for being who she was.

On the ride home with her father, he told her it had been "the last straw." She was not even seven at the time and had no idea what that meant. She had used a straw at the hospital, and she wondered if it meant she would not be allowed to drink from a straw anymore.

But as he explained more, she realized it meant she'd no longer be going to school. He was going to enroll her in correspondence courses at home. They had tried the boarding school, he recalled to her. Lilac felt sick when he mentioned that school, and she wanted him to stop talking about it immediately, hoping he wouldn't go into details. Then he reminded her of the school for the gifted, and the cruel girls there that had caused Lilac so much panic, her father had to pull her out and hire a private tutor. But the private tutor couldn't handle the ghosts. They had actually gone through three of them, her father reminded her, Susan, Antoinette, and finally, Gregory Allen. And all of this had been quite a bother for him, he noted, and a distraction to his work.

So it would be correspondence courses for Lilac Skully, and she would remain at home in Skully Manor.

She was relieved, in a way, to never have to see Hazel and Finn ever again. But Lilac Skully was going to miss a lot of things about going to the public school. The kind teacher. The one girl who had been friendly to her. The things she'd learned and books they had in the library. The chance to be normal.

As Lilac Skully sat in the car that night, the fresh red stitches throbbed on her pale skin and quite visibly beneath her strange white hair. The chance to be normal was over, she realized. Because she was never going to be normal. She was a Skully.

And she knew her father was probably right. She'd be better off if she just stayed inside the manor, and didn't talk to anyone, ever, at all.

16.
Lilac's Last Chance

Suddenly she wasn't sure if she was still in the lunchroom or back in real life right now. Her head hurt the same either way, she thought. She peeked one eye open just a crack and saw the tile floor of Skully Manor's foyer.

She was here. Now.

She felt the sore side of her head, wet with blood. What had happened? How much time had passed?

Last she remembered, the basement door was locked, and she'd trapped one of the intruders in there. She looked at the door. It was wide open. The other one had come up behind her and knocked her out, she realized.

"Meow?"

She heard a familiar feline and Casper rubbed his head against her hand. She pet him for a moment while lying on the floor.

Crash. She heard from below. *Whiiiiir.*

She sat up and looked around. Her bag of tools and papier-mâché fruit had been strewn all over. She didn't see her sword. She saw her walkie-talkie a few feet away and scrambled on her knees to grab it.

Beep. "Bram?" she called into the walkie-talkie. "Where are you guys! Bram? Milly?" But there was no response.

Bang. Crash. Boom. She heard more noises downstairs, clambering and yelling and the familiar "whir" sound of the orb.

She heard the voice of Mr. Fright, screaming out.

She got to her feet and looked around the foyer. She grabbed a very large brass candlestick that was almost as tall as she was, tossed the candle off the top, and followed the crashing sounds down into the basement.

"Mr. Fright?" she called out. But it was too late. Lilac watched as the last bit of Mr. Fright was sucked up into the portable orb's suction hose. His voice faded out in a haunting, wailing, echoing tone—his face contorted as the last of it swirled down the tube. Lilac was taken aback when she saw him press up against the glass, a look of terror, fear, and sadness mixed with the pulse of the horrible electrical shocks that contained the ghosts in the orb. From inside the orb, Mr. Fright locked eyes with Lilac and pleaded to her silently for help.

"We got him!" the two men shouted at each other and high-fived, whooping and hollering. They still hadn't seen Lilac at the bottom of the stairs.

"We got all three!" the other man yelled. They exchanged a few more excited words and switched off the whirring suction of their portable orbs.

"All three?" Lilac repeated to herself and paused, trying to comprehend what they were saying.

A terrible wave of knowing caught Lilac straight in the gut with what she saw next. Pressed against the glass of the orb on the far side of the cellar were the faces of Milly and Bram.

Lilac stifled her horror and charged, catching the men off guard. She lifted the large brass candlestick over her head, took two leaps forward and smashed the top of the closest orb as hard as she could.

Smash. She was pretty sure it was the same orb she'd already hit once with the sword, as the thick glass could not take the force of the blow from the candlestick and shattered.

"Bwaaaaaahahahah!" Mr. Fright's maniacal laugh echoed through the basement as he escaped from the cracks in the orb. Lilac cheered. She saw her sword nearby on the ground and ran for it.

"It's that blasted little girl" one of the men yelled.

"That's our ghost!" the other shouted as Mr. Fright disappeared through the wall. "He's getting away!"

"Get that little girl!" the man on the ground yelled. "Get her!"

She turned as quickly as she could with the brass candlestick in one hand and the sword in the other. She ran for the stairs. Once halfway up she threw the heavy candlestick backward to slow them down. She slammed the door shut behind her at the top, and locked it. She knew it wouldn't contain them long, but it gave her a moment to think.

"Think!" she stood in the foyer again and froze. "Think, think, think!" She hit the sides of her head, trying to jostle her brain. It was not working. She could not think. The men were banging on the door and rattling the handle. *Bang.* She heard them using the large brass candlestick to try to smash their way in. *Bang. Bang. Bang.*

"That was a pretty good *whack* in the cellar with the candlestick, Little Girl Skully!" Mr. Fright's creepy voice called out behind her.

"Mr. Fright!" she exclaimed, never so happy to see him in all of her life. "You've got to help me now," she demanded and crossed her arms, folding them in front of her and narrowing her eyes. "That's twice I've got you out of the orb, and there won't be a third time unless..."

He cut her off. "Oh, I'll help you, little girl!" Mr. Fright laughed in his sick, twisted way, much too jovially for the seriousness of the situation.

"We'll get back at them now!" he cackled, "With a vengeance!" He looked up and to the side, wiggling his fingers together excitedly as dastardly plans rolled through his mind.

"We need to try to break the other orb," Lilac explained to him, "and free Milly and Bram."

Bang! With a loud bang, the candlestick finally broke through the door, and one of the men's arms reached through and unlocked the doorknob.

"Here!" Lilac pulled out a pair of red-handled wire cutters from her bag and tossed them to Mr. Fright. He caught them and then disappeared instantly. The intruders bashed through the door. Lilac ran.

"Get her!" the men yelled. She could feel the wind of their breath and movement just a half step behind her as she ran to the stairs.

Hop! Lilac jumped over the last step to miss the trip wire. She sped down the Hall of the Little Girl Ghost as quickly as she could.

"Aaah!" She heard one of them yell, and turned her head back to look.

The first man up the stairs had hit the trip wire and had fallen flat on his face. The second man couldn't stop himself and landed on top. Lilac looked back just in time to see a pair of red-handled wire cutters float through the air and snip some of the wires on the orb they were still dragging through the manor, the one that held Milly and Bram.

The two men struggled to their feet. Lilac counted down.

Three. Two. One. She said under her breath. She sliced a rope with the sword.

Clang. The knight's arm on the old suit of armor swung down, butcher knife in hand.

"Oh god!" She heard one of the men cry out again in pain.

Lilac wanted to see if she'd hit him and made him bleed but wasted no time. She darted up the stairs to the third floor and up the next flight to the attic tower, and prepared herself at the top.

As soon as the men got to the bottom of the stairs, Lilac launched the first bowling ball. She held it with both hands and swung it between her knees, using as much force as she could.

"You guys like bowling?" she yelled maniacally, not knowing exactly what she was saying or why.

Bang. Bang. Bang. It went with increasing speed at each step.

She launched another. *Bang. Bang. Bang.*

"Damn this little girl!" she heard one say to the other. "Let's just get out of here!"

"We need that gear, Jerry! And she knows where it is!" The anger and frustration in the men's voices were rising.

Bang. Bang. Bang. She launched another bowling ball. It didn't seem to be working. She heard the men continue to step up the stairs, dragging the portable orb behind them.

The two men were quite large, and they completely blocked the stairs back down, the only exit Lilac had.

"Just tell us where you hid the gear, little girl, and we'll leave."

"I didn't hide any gear!" Lilac yelled back at them.

"Where'd it go then, huh?" one of them said back. "Did a ghost take it? I don't think so!"

"Someone else came in and stole it because you broke my cellar door." Lilac retorted. She was not going to take this anymore. This was her house.

Snip! She heard from behind the men and tried not to flinch or draw any attention to Mr. Fright.

"What was that?" one of them said and turned around. Lilac's heart sank but then noticed he had taken off his ghost goggles and set them on his forehead, so he probably hadn't seen Mr. Fright floating there right behind them.

"I'll show you where I hid the gear," Lilac said quickly. "If you promise to leave."

The men turned around and took a few steps toward her.

"Where?" one of them said with a glare.

"Up there," Lilac said, and pointed up.

"Up where?" the angry man demanded.

"Up on the rafters." Lilac said.

And she pointed up to a board of plywood laid over the rafters ten feet up in the tall, pointed tower attic. Lots of attics had rafters with boards like this, for people to store things on top of them.

"How'd a little girl get all that heavy gear way up there?" one of the men asked skeptically.

"The ghosts helped me," Lilac said, calmly and plainly.

The man laughed. "You expect us to believe that?" he snickered.

"Why not!" she quipped. "I'm a Skully, aren't I?"

"Well, tell the ghosts to get them back down, Skully!" the other man exclaimed, the one Lilac had knocked out with the pet cemetery grave marker.

"How can I do that if you've captured the ones that helped me?" Lilac barked, crossing her arms at his stupidity. "You'll either have to let the ghosts out or use that rickety old ladder and climb up there yourself!" She pointed at an ancient hand-made ladder propped against the wall.

The first man scoffed at her and went to grab the ladder, frustrated, injured, and not wanting to waste any more time arguing with a little girl about ghosts. He brought it to the middle of the attic and propped it up, so the top rungs were set against the rafters high above.

"Hold this ladder," he said impatiently to the other man.

He started up the ladder as the other man held the bottom. The entire ladder bent and flexed with each step he took.

Lilac waited until he had gone almost all the way up to the top, but before he could see over into the loft.

Three. Two. One. She abandoned her sword, as nonchalantly as she could, and darted forward, grabbing the handle of the portable orb and yanking it back towards the stairs. Even with two hands and with wheels on the bottom, it was so heavy, she could barely drag it across the floor.

"Hey!" She heard the man holding the ladder yell as he realized what she was doing. The man at the top looked down.

"Stop her!" the man on the top yelled. The man holding the ladder let go and went after Lilac. The ladder instantly went wibbly-wobbly and started to topple with the man still on top.

"No! Don't let go of the ladder, you idiot!" he yelled.

The man at the bottom stopped mid-run and turned back to the ladder, but it was too late. The ladder fell backward with a slow motion fall, the man hanging onto it for dear life, uselessly, as he fell back.

"Whooooa nooo!" he yelled as he went down.

Boom. The ladder fell on top of the man who was trying to catch it, pinning him underneath.

In the free moment created by the chaos, Lilac tipped the box of the portable orb on its side. She looked down and saw Milly and Bram's faces staring back up at her. She nodded to them and slid the orb to the edge of the stairs, and climbed on top.

Holding onto both sides, she scooted the rectangular box and orb forward till it tipped over the first stair and started to slide down.

"Whoooooooa!" Lilac Skully yelled as she rode down the stairs on top of the orb. It went faster and farther than she had expected. She was thrown into the hallway on the third floor with a big thump.

Lilac scrambled back to it and unscrewed the hose.

"Milly! Bram!" she called to them inside, but they were still trapped.

She opened the control panel on the back. There were various switches with tiny markings and letters. Lilac tried to decipher what they meant, but a lot of them were in code or symbols.

"Reverse!" she cried out and flicked the switch marked as such, just as the men started back down the stairs. The machine whirred a bit and sputtered.

"Try it now, guys!" she yelled again, as the ghosts tried to push their way out but were still trapped. They shook their heads. She tried all of the other buttons and switches, pulling at the wires and doing what she could to open the orb.

The men reached the bottom of the stairs.

"Get her, Jerry!" She heard one of them yell.

Bleep! Flooop.

Lilac finally hit the right combination of switches when she twisted a yellow knob marked "Release Hatch" in teeny-tiny letters, and flicked the reverse switch back up and down again. The orb finally went into reverse, ejecting the ghosts of Milly and Bram with a cold, musty swoosh.

"Get out of here!" Lilac yelled to them, as she began to stomp and smash the orb to try to break it.

"Allow me, Little Girl Skully!" Mr. Fright swooped in and picked up the orb, flying it down the staircase away from the grasp of the men.

Lilac ran. She slid down the banister to the second floor, and then again down to the first. She hopped off and flew through the air at the bottom as she had done so many times.

She landed in the center of the foyer and gasped.

Someone was standing in the foyer.

It was the police.

17.

Doomed

Lilac froze. This was it. She was doomed. The impending scene raced through her head. Her father in jail. Skully Manor up for auction. She would be with a guardian that insisted that she participate in team sports and other outdoor activities because they would be good for her, taking her away from her beloved reading time.

The officer tried to talk to her, but she did not respond.

"Easy there," the officer said. It was Officer Grimble, the woman from the day before. "It's okay, I'm here to help," she said. "What's your name?"

Lilac's horror was broken by the sound of the men clambering down the stairs after her, unknowing of the presence of the police.

"Get her, Jerry!" the man that wasn't named Jerry called as they ran downstairs, two steps at a time.

Officer Grimble stepped out into the foyer of Skully Manor and switched on the lights.

The men froze on the stairs at the sight of Office

Grimble. Everyone fell silent. The sound of sirens in the distance grew nearer.

Lilac gulped. "They broke into my house," she finally said, ever so quietly.

The intruders tried to run back upstairs and evade capture from Officer Grimble, but Officer Grimble was too fast. She was able to handcuff and detain both of them until her backup arrived to haul them off.

Lilac was hoping she'd be able to disappear and hide during all the commotion. She slipped around the corner of the dining hall and thought she might be able to escape and be forgotten, but Officer Grimble's voice called out again.

"Not so fast there, dear," The officer reached out and touched Lilac's shoulder, firmly yet gently. Lilac couldn't remember the last time anyone had reached out to her gently. A part of her wanted to turn around and hug Officer Grimble, to run into her arms. But instead she sat down under the dining table and out of the officer's reach, the other part of her hoping to disappear, wishing she could be just like Milly and fade out of sight.

"Do you live here?" Officer Grimble asked.

Lilac wanted to lie and say no, but she couldn't lie. Her head nodded.

"Where are your parents?" Officer Grimble asked.

Lilac stuttered. "I... I don't know!"

It was true. Lilac didn't know. Well, she knew that her mother had died and that her father was somewhere, probably at Black, Black and Gremory Laboratories, but she wasn't actually sure about that. And she didn't really know where you go when you die, so Lilac was telling the truth to Officer Grimble.

Officer Grimble stood for a moment and thought about what to do with Lilac.

A chilly unsettling breeze blew in from the manor, and Lilac got a whiff of a pale, sweet scent. It was the breeze and scent that Lilac Skully knew all too well. It was a sign that the ghosts were haunting.

Lilac inhaled.

"Thank you, Officers!" a strange, eerie voice called out from the foyer. Lilac sat forward, perplexed.

It was not her father's voice or figure, but it was someone—or something—and it was wearing her father's coat, hat, scarf, pants, gloves, and boots. The scarf was wrapped around his face, and the hat pulled down over his eyes.

"Thank you so much for apprehending those thieves and saving my daughter, Lilac, from being kidnapped." the strange figure in her father's clothes said.

Lilac was about to protest that it wasn't her father, but the figure looked at her sharply and cut her off.

"I don't know what I'd do if something happened to my dear Lilac..." the figure said again, looking at her straight in the eyes.

Lilac's eyes locked with his. She knew those eyes. It was Mr. Fright.

"I am Dr. Skully, Officer..." He paused quizzically as if to ask for the officer's name.

"Officer Grimble," she replied, reaching out a hand to shake.

Mr. Fright's figure let out a sudden cough and put his gloved hands in the coat pockets. "I'm... recovering from influenza!" He coughed again. "Yes, yes..." he coughed louder. "Terrible influenza!"

Lilac thought he might be overdoing it, but she stayed silent.

"So," Mr. Fright explained. "I was resting deeply and did not hear the commotion tonight."

"Oh, it's our duty to protect the citizens of Steamville, such as yourself, Dr. Skully," Officer Grimble replied.

"Since I'm not well," Mr. Fright coughed again for effect, then continued, "I'd like to sign any paperwork necessary to press charges against these men for breaking and entering, and get back to bed." He nodded at Officer Grimble. "I'll deal with the insurance and the damage done to my property tomorrow. Hopefully, I'll be feeling a bit better by then."

"Of course, Dr. Skully, right this way, sir, we'll get you all set and be on our way quickly." Officer Grimble motioned for him to walk out into the foyer.

Mr. Fright turned back and winked at Lilac from under the hat.

Lilac sat motionless under the large dining table. She watched as Officer Grimble had Mr. Fright sign a few pieces of paper. She saw the police drag out the two intruders in handcuffs. She saw Mr. Fright decline when the officers asked to come in for further investigation. She watched as Mr. Fright waved goodnight and shut the front door of Skully Manor.

Everything was silent for a moment. Mr. Fright turned and took three steps through the foyer. He stopped. He looked at Lilac Skully, still hiding under the table. She smiled at him.

"Th... thanks," Lilac said to Mr. Fright.

Just then the figure in her father's clothing disappeared, and the clothes slunk down into a pile on the floor. The hat sat right on top of the shoes, pants, coat, and scarf.

Lilac got up and ran over. "Mr. Fright?" she called. But there was no response. She felt a chill running up her spine and down her arms. A warm breeze rushed through Skully Manor. Then a soft white glow and a column of light appeared over the clothes and extended from floor to ceiling in the foyer.

"Mr. Fright?" Lilac called softly, her eyes unable to move from the twinkling, warm column of light. Tiny flickers of dust, like fairies, were jumping in and out, in all colors of the rainbow.

"It's too late, Lilac," she heard a familiar voice call from upstairs. She looked up to see the ghost of Milly, hovering at the top of the stairs.

"Milly!" Lilac exclaimed in excitement.

"Mr. Fright's passed on," Milly said solemnly, her hand outstretched to the beam of light. "He's gone."

18.
The End

"Passed on?" Lilac stammered. "I thought he was already... gone?" She didn't understand.

"Into the light, Lilac," Milly tried to explain. "To another realm beyond," Her hand reached out again, and she floated smoothly down the stairs.

Lilac looked back at the pile of clothes where Mr. Fright stood just a moment ago. The column of glimmering light was now so dim, Lilac wondered if she had seen it at all.

"I don't understand?" Lilac asked. She didn't.

"We're here for reasons, you know," Milly said to Lilac. "Lots of reasons. But there comes a time to leave, and I guess you never know what it'll take for that time to come..." She motioned upwards where the light had been. "And move on..." she said, forlornly. "To the beyond..."

"So what happened to Mr. Fright? Why was it time for him to leave? Where'd he go?" Lilac still didn't understand.

"I believe I might know." A figure appeared from the

darkness upstairs. It was Bram. "It's no secret that Mr. Fright hated little girls," Bram explained to Lilac. "And thoroughly enjoyed haunting them." Bram couldn't help but smile at this memory. "Until the day that he didn't." He said more seriously.

Lilac still didn't understand. "Until the day he didn't what?" she asked.

"Till the day he didn't hate little girls anymore, Miss Skully. And I'm guessing this had to do with you." Bram replied.

Lilac stared at him, brow furrowed.

"Oh it's not a bad thing," Bram said softly. "Yes, he'll be missed, strangely, by all who haunt here at Skully Manor." He nodded and raised his eyebrows, "But now he's free. And may his soul be at rest. After a very long time of haunting here, I might add." With this, Bram became emotional and dabbed his eyes.

Lilac still must have had a confused look on her face because Bram continued.

"You saved him once, Lilac Skully, from the horrible orb." He locked his gaze with Lilac and continued. "And then you saved him again tonight." He nodded, but Lilac was still not catching on. "And in turn, he saved you," Bram continued. "And I think it was then that he realized he had no further reason to haunt this earth... if he no longer found joy in haunting little girls," Bram could not continue. He began to cry quietly into his handkerchief.

"I... I'm so sorry!" Lilac gasped, thinking she'd done something terribly wrong.

"No, no, no, Miss Skully," Bram blew his nose into a handkerchief. "It's quite alright. It's bittersweet. We'll all go at some point, and he had a good haunt."

Lilac felt terrible. She had just started to like Mr. Fright.

"I wanted to save you all!" she said to the ghosts. She was not expecting this. She thought the ghosts would be there forever.

"You did save us," Milly said, even though her brother had been captured and was still held captive somewhere. She floated towards Lilac. "Mr. Fright's better off now," Milly said in a gloomy voice. "It's hard to go, but he'll be reborn, well, I believe that, anyway."

Lilac's head tilted.

"It's actually kind of exciting," Milly added. "Many say that it's a new beginning." Her face shifted a bit, "Some say it's the end of all ends..." She smiled and looked back up at Lilac. "But I guess it depends on who you ask..."

Lilac picked up all of her father's clothes and brought them back to his room. As soon as she opened the door, she paused. She hadn't been in his room in years. She couldn't remember how long it had been. It almost seemed too personal, as if she was intruding, and she hurried to fold the clothes and set them down nicely on the bed.

Then a picture on the bedside table caught her eye. It was a strange but beautiful woman with bright white hair, large dark eyes and a sly half smile. It was her mother. Lilac stared at the photograph. Her mother seemed to be looking right at her, like she had been watching Lilac before Lilac had noticed her in the photo. And now Lilac couldn't look away. She realized she never knew there was a photo of her mother there. She thought her father didn't have any out at all. But there she was. Her mother. Lilac broke her trance and hurried out of her father's room, closing the door behind her.

She went back to the foyer and found the large candlestick that she'd used as a weapon, and set it back up, putting the candle back on top. She tried to clean up some of the burned and charred items from her séance, which felt so long ago, although it had only been a couple of days. She picked up the burnt remnants of her purple book, *How to Deal With Ghosts*. She had liked that book, but she supposed there was no use for it anymore.

Lilac dragged the large and grotesque crest of the house of Skully back to the second floor landing, step by step. She lowered it back over the banister till it hung where it had been for four generations. The large crest emblazoned with real human skulls and bones—as legend had it. And the crest of the House of Skully hung once more over the grand foyer.

"To House Skully!" she said, lifting her sword skyward.

Lilac went to place her sword back in the sheath that hung over the crest, but changed her mind. She'd better keep it close by, just in case, she thought.

Lilac put a few more things away and then noticed that dawn was starting to break outside.

"Well. I'm getting tired," she yawned. "I guess I'll go to bed." She looked around. The ghosts had vanished, and she was in the foyer alone. She went back to the maid's quarters and got her warmest down blanket. "Come on, Casper," she said to her cat, who was sleeping on the window seat, wondering what she was doing.

Lilac flicked off the lights in the kitchen and slipped through Skully Manor, the corner of her blanket dragging silently behind her. Casper followed.

She climbed the stairs and went into her bedroom, then flicked on the lights. She put the blanket back on her bed and patted it for Casper to jump up. He did.

"Goodnight, Milly," Lilac said.

"Goodnight, Lilac," Milly replied as her apparition appeared in the hall.

Lilac turned off the light and crawled into her bed.
“Milly?” she said after a few moments of silence.
“Yeah?” Milly replied.
“I’m glad we’re friends.”

A Note from Amy:

Dear Reader, I hope you enjoyed *Lilac Skully and the Haunted House!* I also grew up in a house that was over one hundred years old—just like Skully Manor. My house wasn't haunted but it still had its share of creepy, quirky, and spooky qualities, some of which inspired parts of this book.

There are two things you might have noticed in this story—one is that Skully Manor has a third floor where Lilac doesn't go, other than passing up the staircase on the way to the attic tower. The other thing you may have noticed is that Lilac didn't really leave the manor at all. And it turns out she hasn't left in quite a while.

But all of this is about to change as Lilac steps out of the house on a haunted adventure that she won't forget.

Don't miss Book #2, *Lilac Skully and the Carriage of Lost Souls!*

And if you'd like to leave a review of this book and share your thoughts with other readers, it would be much appreciated.

Thanks for reading!

Amy Cesari

THE STORY CONTINUES IN LILAC'S 2ND BOOK!

Lilac Skully and the Carriage of Lost Souls

Available now in paperback and eBook.

Would you take a ride in the Carriage of Lost Souls?

Lilac Skully knows she's in grave danger. And she's determined to do something about it.

The only living soul in Skully Manor (other than her cat), nine-year-old Lilac comes up with a daring plan to find her father. But when she travels to the world of the dead, she discovers more danger and darkness than she could've imagined. Not all ghosts are friendly, and Lilac's heroic rescue efforts turn into a grim reality that she may not escape.

Join Lilac on a haunting adventure as she finds the courage to leave Skully Manor, face her foes, and make new friends.

★★★★★

"The *Carriage of Lost Souls* is original, fun and suspenseful, I couldn't put it down. I can't wait to see what's next for Lilac and her supernatural friends."

"Lilac is the bravest scaredy-cat, and it's perfection. These books are adorably creepy, my child and I love to read about Lilacs adventures! They aren't too scary and hold a few good lessons learned in each book. Lilac is a great role model for anyone trying to find their way, we can't wait to read the next installment!"

The Lilac Skully Series

Book 1: Lilac Skully and the Haunted House
Book 2: Lilac Skully and the Carriage of Lost Souls
Book 3: Lilac Skully and the Halloween Moon
Book 4+: (forthcoming)

About the Author

Amy Cesari is an author and illustrator who lives in an enchanted forest. She enjoys growing pumpkins in the summer, crocheting in the winter, and watching cartoons year-round. She believes in magic and in the power of following your own creativity. And she has every Nintendo game console ever made, plus a vintage Ms. PacMan arcade machine.

You can contact Amy at: amy@lilacskully.com or visit LilacSkully.com for a spooky surprise.

Made in the USA
Middletown, DE
23 May 2019